William Clark Russell

My Danish Sweetheart

A novel

William Clark Russell

My Danish Sweetheart
A novel

ISBN/EAN: 9783337045647

Printed in Europe, USA, Canada, Australia, Japan

Cover: Foto ©Andreas Hilbeck / pixelio.de

More available books at **www.hansebooks.com**

MY DANISH SWEETHEART

A Novel

BY

W. CLARK RUSSELL

AUTHOR OF

'THE WRECK OF THE GROSVENOR,' 'THE LIFE OF ADMIRAL LORD COLLINGWOOD,'
'A MARRIAGE AT SEA,' ETC., ETC.

IN THREE VOLUMES

VOL. I.

Methuen & Co.

18, BURY STREET, LONDON, W.C.

1891

CONTENTS OF VOL. I.

MY DANISH SWEETHEART.

CHAPTER I.

A SULLEN DAY.

ON the morning of October 21, in a year that one need not count very far back to arrive at, I was awakened from a light sleep into which I had fallen after a somewhat restless night by a sound as of thunder some little distance off, and on going to my bedroom window to take a view of the weather I beheld so wild and forbidding a prospect of sea and sky that the like of it is not to be imagined.

The heavens were a dark, stooping, universal mass of vapour—swollen, moist, of a complexion rendered malignant beyond belief by a sort of greenish colour that lay upon the face of it. It was tufted here and there into the true aspect of the electric tempest ; in other parts, it was of a sulky, foggy thickness ; and as it went down to the sea-line it wore, in numerous places, a plentiful dark shading that caused the clouds upon which this darkness rested to look as though their heavy burthen of thunder was weighing their overcharged breasts down to the very sip of the salt.

A small swell was rolling in betwixt the two horns of cliff which framed the wide bight of bay that I was overlooking. The water was very dark and ugly with its reflection of the greenish, sallowish atmosphere that tinged its noiseless, sliding volumes. Yet spite of the shrouding shadow of storm all about, the horizon lay a clear line, spanning the yawn of ocean and heaven betwixt the foreland points.

There was nothing to be seen seaward ; the bay, too, was empty. I stood for a little while watching the cloud of foam made by the swell where it struck upon the low, black ledge of what we call in those parts Deadlow Rock, and upon the westernmost of the two fangs of reef, some little distance away from the Rock, and named by the sailors hereabouts the Twins ; I say I stood watching this small play of white water and hearkening for another rumble of thunder ; but all remained hushed—not a breath of air—no glance of dumb lightning.

On my way to the parlour I looked in upon my mother, now an old lady, whose growing infirmities obliged her to keep her bed till the day was advanced. I kissed and greeted her.

' It seems a very dark melancholy morning, Hugh,' says she.

' Ay, indeed,' I answered. ' I never remember the like of such a sky as is hanging over the water. Did you hear the thunder just now, mother ?'

She answered no, but then, to be sure, she was a little deaf.

' I hope, Hugh,' said she, with a shake of her head and smoothing her snow-white hair with a hand that slightly trembled, ' that it may not end in a life-boat errand. I had a wretched dream last night. I saw you enter the boat and sail into the bay. The sun was high and all was bright and clear ; but on a sudden the weather grew black—dark as it now is. The wind swept the water, which leaped high and

boiled. You and the men strove hard to regain the
land, and then gave up in despair, and you put right
before the wind, and the boat sped like an arrow
into the gloom and haze ; and just before she vanished
a figure rose by your side where you sat steering, and
gazed at me thus '—she placed her forefinger upon
her lip in the posture of one commanding silence. ' It
was your father, Hugh : his face was full of entreaty
and despair.' She sighed deeply. ' How clearly does
one sometimes see in dreams !' she added. ' Never
was your father's face in his dear life more distinct to
my eyes than in this vision.'

' A Friday night's dream told on a Saturday !' said
I, laughing ; ' no chance of its coming true, though.
No fear of the *Janet*'—for that was the name of our
lifeboat—' blowing out to sea. Besides, the bay is
empty. There can be no call. And supposing one
should come and this weather should burst into a
hurricane, I'd rather be afloat in the *Janet* than in
the biggest ship out of London or Liverpool docks ;'
and so saying I left her, never giving her dream or
her manner another thought.

After I had breakfasted I walked down to the

esplanade to view the *Janet* as she lay snug in her house. I was her coxswain, and how it happened that I filled that post I will here explain.

My father, who had been a captain in the merchant service, had saved money, and invested his little fortune in a couple of ships, in one of which, fifteen years before the date of this story, he had embarked to take a run in her from the river Thames to Swansea, where she was to fill up with cargo for a South American port. She was a brand-new ship, and he wished to judge of her sea-going qualities. When she had rounded the North Foreland the weather thickened; it came on to blow a gale of wind; the vessel took the ground somewhere near the North Sand Head, and of twenty-three people aboard of her fifteen perished, my father being among those who were drowned.

His brother—my uncle, George Tregarthen—was a well-to-do merchant in the City of London, and in memory of my father's death, which grieved him to the soul, and which, with the loss of the others, had come about through delay in sending help from the land—for they fired guns and burnt flares, and the

adjacent light-ship signalled with rockets that a
vessel was ashore ; but all to no purpose, for when
the rescue was attempted the ship was breaking up,
and most of her people were corpses, as I have said
—my uncle, by way of memorializing his brother's
death, at his own cost presented the little town in
which my father had lived with a lifeboat, which he
called the *Janet*, after my mother.   I was then too
young to take a part in any services she rendered ;
but by the time I had reached the age of twenty I
was as expert as the smartest boatman on our part
of the coast, and as I claimed a sort of captaincy of
the lifeboat by virtue of her as a family gift, I
replaced the man who had been her coxswain, and for
the last two years had taken her helm during the six
times she had been called upon ; and not a little
proud was I to be able to boast that, under my
charge, the *Janet* in those two years had rescued
twenty-three men, five women, and two children from
certain death.

No man could love his dog or his horse—indeed, I
may say, no man could love his sweetheart—with
more fondness than I loved my boat.   She was a

living thing, to my fancy, even when she was high and dry. She- seemed to appeal to me out of a vitality that might well have passed for human, to judge of the moods it kindled in me. I would sit and view her, and think of her afloat, figure some dreadful scene of shipwreck, some furious surface of seething yeast, with a ship in the heart of it, coming and going amid storms of spray; and then I would picture the boat crushing the savage surge with her shoulder, as she stormed through the tremendous play of ocean on her way to the doomed craft whose shrouds were thick with men; until such emotions were raised in me that I have known myself almost unconsciously to make an eager step to the craft, and pat her side, and talk to her as though she were living and could understand my caress and whispers.

My mother was at first strongly opposed to my risking my life in the *Janet.* She said I was not a sailor, least of all was I of the kind who manned these boats, and for some time she would not hear of me going as coxswain in her, except in fine weather or when there was little risk. But when, as coxswain,

I had brought home my first little load of precious
human freight—five Spaniards, with the captain's
wife and a little baby, wrapped in a shawl, against
her heart—my mother's reluctance yielded to her
pride and gratitude. She found something beautiful,
noble, I had almost said divine, in this life-saving—
in this plucking of poor human souls from the horrible
jaws of Death—in the hope and joy, too, raised in the
heart of the shipwrecked by the sight of the boat, or
in the supporting animation which came from knowledge that the boat would arrive in time, and which
enabled men to bear up, when, perhaps, had there
been no promise of a boat coming to them, they
must have drooped and surrendered their spirits to
God.

Well, as I have said, I went down to the esplanade,
where the boat-house was, to take a look at the boat,
which was, indeed, my regular daily custom, one I
could find plenty of leisure for, since I was without
occupation, owing to a serious illness that had baulked
my efforts six years before, and that had left me too
old for another chance in the same way—and without
will, either, for the matter of that ; for my mother's in-

come was abundant for us both, and, when it should please God to take her, what was hers would be mine, and there was more than enough for my plain wants.

Before entering the house I came to a stand to light a pipe and cast a look around. The air was so motionless that the flame of the match I struck burnt without a stir. I took notice of a slight increase in the weight of the swell which came brimming into the bay out of the wide, dark field of the Atlantic Ocean: for that was the sea our town faced, looking due west from out of the shadow of the Cornwall heights, at the base of which it stood—a small, solid heap of granite-coloured buildings dominated by the tall spire of the church of St. Saviour, the gilt cross atop of which gleamed this morning against the scowl of the sky as though the beam of the risen sun rested upon it.

The dark line of the broad esplanade went winding round with the trend of shore to the distance of about a mile. The dingy atmosphere gave it a colouring of chocolate, and the space of white sand which stretched to the wash of the water had the glance of ivory from the contrast. The surf was small, but now that I was

near I could catch a note in the noise of it as it
foamed in a cloudy line upon the sand, which made
me think of the voice of a distant tempest, as though
each running fold brought with it, from far past the
sea-line, some ever-dying echo of the hurricane's rage
there. But a man had need to live long at the sea-
side to catch these small accents of storm in the fall
and pouring of the unvexed breaker.

A number of white-breasted gulls, with black-edged
wings, were flying close inshore this side the Deadlow
Rock and Twins : their posture was in the main one
of hovering and peering, and there was a sort of
subdued expectancy rather than restlessness in their
motions ; but they frequently uttered sharp cries, and
were certainly not afishing, for they never stooped.
Within a stone's-throw of the lifeboat house was
a coastguard's hut, a little place for keeping a look-
out from, marked by a flag-post ; and the preventive-
man, with a telescope under his arm, stood in the
doorway, talking to an aged boatman named Isaac
Jordan. The land past that flagstaff went in a rise,
and soared into a very noble height of dark cliff, the
extremity of which we called Hurricane Point. It

looked a precipitous, deadly, inhospitable terrace of
rocks in the dismal light of that leaden morning.
The foreland rose out of the bed of foam which was
kept boiling at the iron base by the steadfast hurl of
the Atlantic swell; yet Hurricane Point made a fine
shelter of our bay when the wind came out from the
north, and I have seen the sea there bursting and
soaring into the air in volumes of steam, and the
water a mile and a half out running wide and wild
and white with the whipping of the gale, when,
within, a wherry might have strained to her painter
without shipping a cupful of water.

There was an old timber pier going into the sea
from off a projection of land, upon the northernmost
point of which the lifeboat house stood ; this pier
had a curl like the crook of a sailor's rheumatic forefinger ; but it was not possible to find any sort of
harbour in the rude, black, gleaming embrace of its
pitched and weedy piles, save in smooth and quiet
weather. It was an old pier, and had withstood the
wash and shocks of fifty years of the Atlantic billow
—enough to justify a man in staring at it, since ours
was a wild and stormy seaboard, where everything

had to be as strong as though we were at sea and had the mighty ocean itself to fight. At times a collier would come sailing round Bishopnose Point, a tall, reddish-hued bluff past Deadlow Rock, and slide within the curve of the pier, and discharge her freight. Here, too, in the seasons might be seen a cluster of fishing-boats, mainly the sharp-ended luggers of Penzance ; but this morning, as I have already said, all was vacant from the horizon to the white sweep of sand—vacant and, in a manner, motionless too, with the quality of stagnation that came into the picture out of the sullen, breathless, gloom-laden atmosphere, nothing stirring, as it seemed, save the heave of the swell, and a few active figures of 'longshoremen down by the pier hauling up their boats high and dry upon the sand, with an eye to what was coming in the weather.

I entered the lifeboat house and killed ten minutes or so in surveying the fabric inside and out, and seeing that everything was in readiness should a call come. A ship's barometer—a good instrument— hung against the wall or bulkhead of the wooden edifice. The mercury was low, with a depression in the surface of the metal itself that was like emphasizing the drop.

Our manner of launching the *Janet* was by means of a strong timber slipway, that went in a pretty sharp declivity from the forefoot of the boat to some fathoms past low-water mark. There could be no better way of getting her water-borne. The sand was flat ; there was little to be done with a heavy boat on such a platform, let us have laid what greased woods or rollers we chose under her keel. But from the elevation of her house she fled, when liberated, like a gull into the rage of the water, topping the tallest comber, and giving herself noble way in the teeth of the deadest of inshore hurricanes.

As I stood at the head of this slipway, looking along it to where it buried itself in the dark and sickly green of the flowing heave of the sea, old Isaac Jordan came slowly away from the coastguardsman and saluted me in a voice that trembled under the burthen of eighty-five years. Such another quaint old figure as this might have been hunted for in vain the whole coast round. His eyes, deep-seated in his head seemed to have been formed of agate, so stained and clouded were they by time, by weather, and, no doubt, by drink. His tall hat was bronzed with wear and exposure, the skin of his face lay like a cobweb upon his lineaments, and when he smiled, he exhibited a single tobacco-stained tooth, which made one think of Deadlow Rock. Isaac did not belong to these parts, yet he had lived in the place for above half a century, having been brought ashore from a wreck in which he had been found, the only occupant, lying senseless upon the deck. When he recovered he was without memory, and for five years could not have told his father's name nor the place he hailed from. When at last recollection returned to him, he was satisfied to remain in the corner of this kingdom on which the ocean, so to speak, had cast him, and for fifty years he had never gone half a mile distant from the town unless seaward, and then never beyond the bay, where he would fish for his own feeding, or ply as a carrier between the shore and such ships as brought up.

'Good-marning, Mr. Tregarthen,' said he in the accent of Whitstable, which was his native place; 'reckon there'll be some work afore ye if so be as this here muckiness ain't agoing to blow away ;' and he turned up his marbled eyes to the sky in a sort of blind groping way.

' I never remember the like of such a morning as this, Isaac,' said I, going down to him that I might not oblige him to strain his poor old trembling voice.

' Lard love ye !' he exclaimed ; ' scores and scores, Mr. Tregarthen. I recollect of just such another marning as this in forty-four ; ay, an' an uglier marning yet in thirty-three. That were the day when the *Kingfisher* went down and drownded all hands saving the dawg.'

' What's going to happen, d'ye think, Isaac ?'

' A gale o' wind, master, but not yet. He's a bracing of himself up, and it'll be all day, I allow, afore he's ready ;' and once again he cast up his agate-like eyes to the sky. ' What's the day o' the month, sir ?' he added with a little briskening up.

' October the 21st, isn't it ?'

' Why, Gor bless me ! yes, an' so it be !' he exclaimed, with a face whose expression was rendered spasmodic by an assumption of joyful thought. ' The hanniversary of Trafalgar, as sure as my name's Isaac !

On this day Lord Nelson was killed. Gor bless me! to think of it! I see him now,' he continued, turning his eyes blindly upon my face. 'There's nothen I forget about him. There's his sleeve lying beautifully pinned agin his breast, and the fin of his decapitated harm a-working full of excitement within ; there's his cocked-hat drawed down ower the green shade as lies like a poor man's plaister upon his forehead ; there's his one eye a-looking through and through a man as though it were a bradawl, and t'other eye, said to be sightless, a-imitating of the seeing one till ye couldn't ha' told which was which for health. There was spunk in the werry wounds of that gent. He carried his losses as if they was gains. What a man! There ain't public-houses enough in this country, to drink to the memory of such a gentleman's health in. There ain't. That's my complaint, master. Not public-houses enough, I says, seeing what he did for this here Britain.'

Though nobody in Tintrenale (as I choose to call the town) in the least degree believed that old Isaac ever saw Lord Nelson, despite his swearing that he was five years old at the time, and that he could recollect his mother hoisting him up in her arms above the heads of the crowd to view the great Admiral— I say, though no man believed this old fellow, yet we all listened to his assurances as though very willing to credit what he said. In truth, it pleased us to believe that there was a man in our little community who with his own eyes had beheld the famous Sailor, and we let the thing rest upon our minds as a sort of honourable tradition, which we would not very willingly have disturbed. However, more went to this talk of Nelson in old Isaac than met the ear ; it was indeed, his way of asking for a drink, and, as he had little or nothing to live upon save what he could collect out of charity, I slipped a couple of shillings into his hand, for which he continued to God-bless me till his voice failed him.

I held my gaze fixed upon the sky for some time, to gather, if possible, the direction in which the great swollen canopy of cloud was moving, that I might know from what quarter to expect the wind when it should arise ; but the sullen greenish heaps of shadow hung over the land and sea as motionless as they were dumb. Not the least loose wing of scud was there to be seen moving. It was a wonderfully breathless heaven of tempestuous gloom, with the sea at its confines betwixt the two points of land looking to lift to it in its central part as though swelled, owing to the illusion of the line of livid shade there, and to a depression on either side, caused by a smoky commingling of the atmosphere with the spaces of water.

While I stood surveying the murky scene, that was gradually growing more dim with an insensible thickening of the air, several drops of rain fell, each as large as a half-crown.

'Stand by now for a flash o' lightning,' old Isaac cried in his trembling voice; 'wance them clouds is ripped up, all the water they hold'll tumble down and make room for the wind!'

But there was no lightning. The rain ceased. The stillness seemed to deepen to my hearing, with a fancy to my consciousness of a closer drawing together of the shadows overhead.

''Tain't so wery warm, neither,' said old Isaac; 'and yet here be as true a tropic show as old Jamaikey herself could prowide.'

Every sound was startlingly distinct—the calls and

cries of the fellows near the pier, as they ran their boats up ; the grit of the keels on the hard sand, like the noise of skates travelling on ice ; the low organ-like hum of the larger surf beating upon the coast past Bishopnose Point ; the rattle of vehicles in the stony streets behind me ; the striking of a church bell —the hoarse bawling of a hawker crying fish : it was like the hush one reads of as happening before an earthquake, and I own to an emotion of awe, and even of alarm, as I stood listening and looking.

I hung about the boat-house for hard upon two hours, expecting every minute to see the white line of the wind sweeping across the sea into the bay ; for by this time I had persuaded myself that what motion there was above was out of the westward ; but in all that time the glass-smooth dark-green surface of the swell was never once tarnished by the smallest breath-ing of air. Only one thing that was absent before I now took notice of : I mean a strange, faint, salt smell, as of seaweed in corruption, a somewhat sickly odour of ooze. I had never tasted the like of it upon the atmosphere here ; what it signified I could not imagine. One of my boat's crew, who had paused to exchange a few words with me about the weather, called it the smell of the storm, and said that it arose from a distant disturbance working through the sea through leagues and leagues, as the dews of the body are discharged through the pores of the skin.

This same man had walked up to the heights near to Hurricane Point to take a view of the ocean, and now told me there was nothing in sight, save just a gleam of sail away down in the north-west, almost swallowed up in the gloom. He was without a glass, and could tell me no more than that it was the canvas of a ship.

'Well,' said I, 'nothing, if it be not steam, is going to show itself in this amazing calm.' And, saying this, I turned about and walked leisurely home.

We dined at one o'clock. We were but two, mother and son ; and the little picture of that parlour arises before me as I write, bringing moisture to my eyes as I recall the dear, good, tender heart never more to be beheld by me in this world—as I see the white hair, the kindly aged face, the wistful looks fastened upon me, and hear the little sighs that would softly break from her when she turned her head to send a glance

through the window at the dark malignant junction
of sea and sky ruling the open between the points
and at the frequent flashing of the foam on those evil
rocks grinning upon the heaving waters, away down to
the southward. I could perceive that the memory of
her dream lay upon her in a sort of shadow. Several
times she directed her eyes from my face to the portrait of my father upon the wall opposite her. Yet
she did not again refer to the dream. She talked of
the ugly appearance of the sky, and asked what the
men down about the pier thought of it.

' They are agreed that it is going to end in a gale of
wind,' I answered.

' There is no ship in the bay,' said she, raising a
pair of gold-rimmed glasses to her eyes and peering
through the window.

' No,' said I ; ' and the sea is bare, saving a single
sail somewhere down in the north-west.'

She smiled, as though at a piece of good news.
There could be no summons for the lifeboat, she
knew, if the bay and the ocean beyond remained
empty.

After dinner, while I sat smoking my pipe close

against the fire—for the leaden colour in the air somehow made the atmosphere feel cold, though we were too far west for any touch of autumnal rawness just yet—and while my mother sat opposite me, poring through her glasses upon a local sheet that told the news of the district for the week past—the Rector of Tintrenale, the Rev. John Trembath, happening to pass our window, which was low-seated, looked in, and, spying the outline of my figure against the fire, tapped upon the glass, and I called to him to enter.

' Well, Mr. Coxswain,' says he, ' how is this weather going to end, pray ?   I hear there's a ship making for this bay.'

' I hope not,' says my mother quietly.

' How far distant is she ?' said I.

' Why,' he answered, ' I met old Roscorla just now. He was fresh from Bishopnose way, and told me that there was a square-rigged vessel coming along before a light air of wind out of the west, and apparently heading straight for this bight.'

' She may shift her helm,' said I, who, though no sailor, had yet some acquaintance with the terms of the sea ; 'there'll be no shelter for her here if it comes on to blow from the west.'

'And that's where it is coming from,' said Mr. Trembath.

'Oh for a little break of the sky—for one brief gleam of sunshine!' cried my mother suddenly, half starting from her chair as if to go to the window. 'There's something in a day of this kind that depresses my heart as though sorrow were coming. Do you believe in dreams, Mr. Trembath?' And now I saw she was going to talk of her dream.

'No,' said he bluntly; 'it is enough to believe in what is proper for our spiritual health. A dream never yet saved a soul.'

'Do you think so?' said I. 'Yet a man might get a hint in a vision, and in that way be preserved from doing a wrong.'

'What was your dream?' said Mr. Trembath, rounding upon my mother ; 'for a dream you have had, and I see the recollection of it working in your face as you look at me.'

She repeated her dream to him.

'Tut ! tut !' cried he ; 'a little attack of indigestion.

A small glass of your excellent cherry brandy would have corrected all these crudities of your slumbering imagination.'

Well, after an idle chat of ten minutes, which yet gave the worthy clergyman time enough to drink to us in a glass of that cherry brandy which he had recommended to my mother, he went away, and shortly afterwards I walked down to the pier to catch a sight of the ship. In all these hours there had been no change whatever in the aspect of the weather. The sky of dark cloud wore the same swollen, moist, and scowling appearance it had carried since the early morn, but the tufted thunder-coloured heaps of vapour had been smoothed out or absorbed by the gathering thickness which made the atmosphere so dark that, though it was scarcely three o'clock in the afternoon, you would have supposed the sun had set. The swell had increased ; it was now rolling into the bay with weight and volume, and there was a small roaring noise in the surf already, and a deeper note yet in the sound of it where it boiled seawards past the points. A light air was blowing, but as yet the water was merely brushed by it into wrinkles which put a new dye into the colour of the ocean—a kind of inky green—I do not know how to convey it. Every glance of foam upon the Twins or Deadlow Rock was like a flash of white fire, so sombre was the surface upon which it played.

Hurricane Point shut out the view of the sea in the north-west, even from the pierhead, and the ship was not to be seen. There was a group of watermen on the look-out, one or two of them members of the life-boat crew ; and among these fellows was old Isaac Jordan, who, as I might easily guess, had drunk out my two shillings. He wore a yellow sou'-wester over his long iron-gray hair, and he lurched from one man to another, with his arm extended and his fingers clawing the air, arguing in the shrill voice of old age, thickened by the drams he had swallowed.

'I tell 'ee there's going to be a airthquake,' he was crying as I approached. 'I recollects the likes of this weather in eighteen hunnerd an' eighteen, and there was a quake at midnight that caused the folks at Faversham to git out of their beds and run into the street ; 'twor felt at Whitstable, and turned the beer o' th' place sour. Stand by for a airthquake, I says.

Here's Mr. Tregarthen, a scholard. The likes of me, as is old enough to be granddad to the oldest of ye all, may raison with a scholard and be satisfied to be put right if so be as he's wrong, when such scow-bankers as you a'n't to be condescended to outside the giving of the truth to ye. And so I says. Mr. Tregarthen——'

But I quietly put him aside.

'No more money for you, Isaac,' said I, 'so far as my purse is concerned, until you turn teetotaler. It is enough to make one blush for one's species to see so old a man——'

'Mr. Tregarthen,' he interrupted, 'you're a gin'man, ain't ye! What have I 'ad? Is a drop o' milk and water going to make ye blush for a man?'

Some of the fellows laughed.

'And how often,' he continued, ' is the hanniversary of the battle o' Trafalgar agoing to come round in a year? Twenty-voorst of October to-day is, and I see him now, Mr. Tregarthen, as I see you—his right fin agoing, his horders upon his breast——'

'Here, come you along with me, Isaac!' exclaimed one of the men, and, seizing the old fellow by the arm, he bore him off.

CHAPTER II.

A NIGHT OF STORM.

I OVERHUNG the rail of the pier, looking down upon the heads of the breakers as they dissolved in white water amid the black and slimy supporters of the structure, and sending a glance from time to time towards the northern headland, out of which, I gathered from the men about me, the ship would presently draw, though no one could certainly say as yet that she was bound for our bay, spite of her heading direct in for the land. A half-hour passed, and then she showed : her bowsprit and jibbooms came forking out past the chocolate-coloured height of cliff, and the suddenness of this presentment of white wings of jibs and staysail caused the canvas to look ghastly for the moment against the dark and drooping smoke-coloured sky that overhung the sea where she was—

as ghastly, I say, as the gleam of froth is when seen at midnight, or a glance of moonshine dropping spear-like through a rift and making a little pool of light in the midst of a black ocean.

I watched her with curiosity. She was something less than three miles distant, and she drew out very stately under a full breast of sail, rolling her three spires—the two foremost of which were clothed to the trucks—with the majesty of a war-ship. We might now make sure that she was bound for the bay, and meant to bring up. The air was still a very light wind, which made a continuous wonder of the mute-ness of the storm-shadow that was overhead; and the vessel, which we might now see was a barque of four hundred tons or thereabouts, floated into the bay very slowly. Her canvas swung as she rolled, and made a hurry of light of her, and one saw the glint of the sails broaden in the brows of the swell which chased .and underran her, so reflective was the water, spite of the small wrinkling of it by the weak draught.

'A furriner,' said a man near me.

'Ay,' said I, examining her through a small but powerful pocket-telescope; 'that green caboose doesn't belong to an Englishman. She's hoisting her colour! Now I have it—a Dane !'

'What does she want to come here for ?' exclaimed another of the little knot of men who had gathered about me. 'Something wrong, I allow.'

'Master drunk, per'aps,' said a third.

'He'll be making a lee zhore of our ugly bit of coast if it comes on to blow from the west'ard, and if not from there, then where else it's coming from who's going to guess ?' exclaimed a gruff old fellow, peering at the vessel under a shaggy, contracted brow.

'Her captain may have a trick of the weather above our comprehension,' said I. 'If the gale's to come out of the north, he'll do well where he lets go his anchor ; but if it's to be the other way about—well, I suppose some of our chaps will advise him. Maybe he has been tempted by the look of the bay ; or he may have a sick or a dead man to land.'

'Perhaps he has a mind to vind us a job to-night zur,' said one of my lifeboat's men.

We continued watching. Presently she began to shorten sail, and the leisurely manner in which the canvas was first clewed up and then rolled up was

assurance enough to a nautical eye that she was not
overmanned. I could distinguish the figure of a
short, squarely-framed man, apparently giving orders
from the top of a long house aft, and I could make
out the figure of another man, seemingly young,
flitting to and fro with a manner of idle restlessness,
though at intervals he would pause and sweep the
town and foreshore with his telescope.

About this time five men launched a swift, powerful
boat of a whaling pattern off the sand on to which it
had been dragged that morning, far beyond high-
water mark.   They ran the little fabric over a line of
well-greased planks or skids, and sprang into her as
her bow met the first roll of water, and in a breath
their oars were out and they were sweeping the boat
towards the barque, making the spray spit from the
stem to the herculean sweep of the blades.   She was
a boat that was mainly used for these errands—for
putting help aboard ships which wanted it—for taking
pilots off and bringing them ashore, and the like.   So
slow was the motion of the barque that she was still
floating into the bay with her anchors at the catheads,
and a few heads of men along the yards furling the

lighter canvas, when the boat dashed alongside of her. When the stranger was about a mile and a half distant from the point of pier which I watched her from, she let go her topsail halliards---she carried single sails--- and a few minutes later her anchor fell, and she swung slowly, with her head to the swell and the light wind.

Scarcely was she straining to the scope of cable that had been paid out, when the boat which had gone to her left her side. The men rowed leisurely; one could tell by the rise and fall of the oars that their errand had proved a disappointment, that there was nothing to be earned, nothing to be done, neither help nor counsel wanted. I walked down to that part of the sands where she would come ashore, but had to wait until her crew had walked her up out of the water before I could get any news. Our town was so dull, our habits of thought so primitive as to be almost childlike—the bay for long spells at a time so barren of all interests, that the arrival of a vessel, if it were not a smack or a collier, excited the sort of curiosity among us that a new-comer raises in a little village. A ship bringing up in the bay was something to look at, something to speculate upon ; and then, again, there was always the expectation among the 'longshoremen of earning a few pounds out of her.

I called to one of the crew of the boat after she had been secured high and dry, and asked him the name of the vessel.

' The *Anine,*' says he.

' What's wrong with her ?' said I.

' Nothing but fear of the weather, I allow,' said he ; ' she's from Cuxhaven, bound to Party Alleggy, or some such a hole away down in the Brazils.'

' Porto Alegre, is it ?' said I.

' Ay,' he answered, ' that zounds nearer to the name that vur given to us. She's got a general cargo aboard. The master's laid up in the cabin ; the chief mate broke un's leg off Texel, and they zent him into Partsmouth aboard of a zmack. The chap in charge calls himself Damm. I onderstood he'z carpenter, acting as zecond mate. But who's to follow such a lingo as he talks ?'

' He's brought up here with the master's sanction, I suppose ?'

'Can't tell you that,' he answered, 'for I don't know. 'Pears to me as if this here traverse was Mr. Damm's own working out. He's got a cross-eye, and I don't rightly like his looks. He pointed aloft and zhook his head, and made us understand that he was here for zhelter. Jimmy,' meaning one of the boat's crew, 'pointed to the Twins, and Mr. Damm he grins and says, " Yaw, yaw, dot's right !" '

' But if he's bound to the Brazils,' I said, 'how does it happen that he is on this side the Land's End ? Porto Alegre isn't in Wales.'

Here another of the boat's crew who had joined us said, ' I understood from a man who spoke a bit of English that they was bound round to Swansea, but what to take in, atop of a general cargo, I can't say.'

The sailors aboard the vessel were now slowly rolling the up canvas upon the yards. She was a wall-sided vessel, with a white figure-head and a square stern, and she pitched so heavily upon the swell sweeping to her bows that one could not but wonder how it would be with her when it came on to blow in earnest, with such a sea as the Atlantic in wrath threw into this rock-framed bight of coast. She rolled as regularly as she curtseyed, and gave us a view of a band of new metal sheathing that rose with a dull rusty gleam out of the water, as though to some swift vanishing touch of stormy sunlight. The white lines of her furled canvas, with the delicate interlacery of shrouds and running-gear, the fine fibres of her slender mastheads with a red spot of dog-vane at the mizzen-mast—the whole body of the vessel, in a word, stood out with an exquisite clearness that made the heaving fabric resemble a choicely wrought toy upon the dark, tempestuous green which went rising and falling past her, and against the low and menacing frown of the sky beyond her.

A deeper shadow seemed to have entered the atmosphere since she let go her anchor. Away down upon her port-quarter the foam was leaping upon the black Twins and the larger rock beyond, and the round of the bay was sharply marked by the surf twisting in a wool-white curve from one point to another, but gathering a brighter whiteness as it stretched towards those extremities of the land which breasted the deeper waters and the larger swell.

The clock of St. Saviour's Church chimed five—
tea-time; and as I turned to make my way home
two bells were struck aboard the barque, and the
light inshore wind brought in the distant tones upon
the ear with a fairy daintiness of faint music that cor-
responded to perfection with the toy-like appearance
of the vessel. One of the crew of the boat accom-
panied me a short distance on his way to his own
humble cottage in Swim Lane.

'If that Dutchman,' said he—and by 'Dutchman'
he meant Dane, for this word covers all the Scandinavian nations in Jack's language—'if that Dutchman,
Mr. Tregarthen, knows what's good for him, he'll up
anchor and "ratch" out afore it's too late.'

'Did you see the captain ?'

'No, sir. He's in his cabin, badly laid up.'

'I thought I made out two men on top of the deck-
house, who seemed in command—one the captain, and
the other the mate, as I supposed.'

'No, sir; the capt'n's below. One of them two
men you saw was the carpenter Damm ; t'other was a
boy—a passenger he looked like, though dressed as a
sailor man. I didn't hear him give any orders, though

his eyes seemed everywhere, and he looked to know exactly what was going forward. A likelier-looking lad I never see. Capt'n's son, I dare say.'

' Well,' said I, sending a glance above and around, 'spite of drunken old Isaac and his prediction of "airthquakes," as he calls them, it's as likely as not, to my mind, that all this gloom will end as it began— in quietude.'

The man—one of the most intelligent of our 'long-shoremen— shook his head.

' The barometer don't tell lies, sir,' said he ; ' the drop's been too slow and regular to signify nothing. I've known a gale o' wind to bust after taking two days to look at the ocean with his breath sucked in, as he do now. This here long quietude's the worst part, and—— Smother me! Mr. Tregarthen,' said he, halting and turning his face seawards, ' if the draught that was just now blowing ain't gone !'

It was as he had said. The light breathing of air had died out, and the swell was rolling in, burnished as liquid glass.

This day-long extraordinary pause in the most menacing aspect of weather that I had ever heard of

—and never in my time had I seen the like of it—
seemed to communicate its own quality of breathless
suspense to every living object my eye rested upon.
The very dogs seemed to move with a cowed manner,
as though fresh from a whipping. There was no
alacrity—little movement, indeed, anywhere visible.
Men hung about in small groups and conversed
quietly, as though some trouble that had affected
the whole community was upon them. The air
trembled with the noise of the breaking surf, and
there was a note in that voice, sounding as it did out of
the unnatural dark hush upon sea and land, that con-
strained the attention to it as to something new and
even alarming. A tradesman, with his apron on and
without a hat, would come to his shop-door and look
about him uneasily, and perhaps have a word with
a customer as he entered before going round the
counter and serving him. The gulls flew close
inshore and screamed harshly. Here and there,
framed in a darkling pane of window, you would
see an old face peering at the weather and pale in the
shadow.

I found my mother a good deal troubled by the

appearance of the ship. She asked, with a pettishness I had seldom witnessed in her, 'What does she want? Why does she come here? Do they court destruction?'

I told her all that I had learnt about the vessel.

'There was no occasion for them to come here,' she said. 'Your dear father would have told you that the more distant a ship is upon the ocean in violent weather the safer she is; and here now come the foolish Danes to nestle among rocks, and to sneer at the advice our people give them, with the sky looking more threatening than ever I can remember it. Who could have patience with such folk?' she cried. pouring out the tea with an air of distraction and an agitated hand. 'If there were no such sailors as they at sea I am sure there would be no need for lifeboats, and brave fellows would not have to risk their lives, and perhaps leave their wives and little children to starve, to assist people whose stupidity renders them almost unfit to be rescued.'

'Why, mother,' cried I, 'this is not how you are accustomed to talk about such things.'

'I am depressed,' she answered; 'my spirits have

taken their colour from the day. A most melancholy
heavy day, indeed! Hark, my dear! Is not that the
sound of wind?'

She looked eagerly, straining her hearing.

'Yes,' said I, 'it is the wind come at last, mother,'
catching, at the instant of her speaking, the hollow
groaning, in the chimney, of a sudden gust of wind
flying over the housetop. 'From which quarter does
it blow? I must find out!'

I ran to the house-door, and as I opened it, the
wind blew with the sweep of a sudden squall right
out of the darkness upon the ocean. It filled the
house, and such was the weight of it that I drove the
door to with difficulty. It was but a quarter before
six, but the shadow of the night had entered to
deepen the shadow of the storm, and it was already
as dark as midnight. I went to the window and
parted the curtains to take a view of the bay, but the
panes of glass were made a sort of mirror of by the
black atmosphere without, and when I looked they
gave me back my own countenance, darkly gleaming,
and the reflection of objects in the room—the lamp
with its green shade upon the table, the sparkle of

the silver and the china of the tea-things, and my
mother's figure beyond. Yet, by peering, I managed
to distinguish the speck of yellow lustre that denoted
the riding light of the Danish barque—the lantern, I
mean, that is hung upon a ship's fore-stay when she
lies at anchor ; otherwise, it was like looking down
into a well. Nothing, save the flash of the near foam
tumbling upon the beach right abreast of the house,
was to be seen.

'Which way does the wind come, Hugh ?' called my
mother.

'From the westward, with a touch of south in it,
too, right dead inshore. It is as I have been expecting all day.'

That night of tempest began in gusts and squalls,
with lulls between, which were not a little deceptive,
since they made one think that the wind was gone for
good, though while the belief was growing there would
come another shrieking outrush and a low roaring in
the chimney, and such a shrill and doleful whistling in
the casements, which there was no art in carpentry to
hermetically seal against the winds of that wild,
rugged western coast, as might have made one

imagine the air to be filled with the ghosts of departed boatswains plying their silver pipes as they sped onwards in the race of black air.

Some while before seven o'clock it had settled into a gale, that was slowly but obstinately gathering in power, as I might know by the gradually raised notes in the humming it made, and by the ever-deepening thunder of warring billows rushing into breakers and bursting upon sand and crag. It came along in a furious play of wet, too, at times; the rain lashed the windows like small shot, and twice there was a brilliant flash of lightning that seemed spiral and crimsoned; but, if thunder followed, it was lost in the uproar of the wind. It was a night to 'stand by,' as a sailor would say; at any moment a summons might come, and, while that weather held, I knew there must be no sleep for me. It would have been all the same, indeed, barque or no barque, for this was a night to make a very hell of the waters along our line of coast; there was not another lifeboat station within twenty-five miles, and, even had the bay been empty, as I say, yet, as coxswain of the boat, I must have held myself ready for a call—ready for the notes

of the bell summoning us to the rescue of a vessel
that had been blown out of the sea into the bay—
ready for a breathless appeal for help from some
mounted messenger despatched by the coastguards
miles distant to tell me that there was a ship stranded
and that all hands must perish if we did not hurry to
her.

My mother sat silent, with her face rendered austere
by anxiety. It was about eight o'clock, when someone
knocked hurriedly at the door. I ran out, being too
eager to await the attendance of the servant ; but, instead of some rough figure of a boatman which I had
expected to see, in swept Mr. Trembath, who was
carried by the violence of the wind several feet along
the passage before he could bring himself up. I put my
shoulder to the door, but believed I should have had
to call for help to close it, so desperate was the
resistance.

'What a night ! What a night !' cried the clergyman. 'What is the news ? You will not tell me,
Tregarthen, that the ship yonder is going to hold
her own against this wind and the sea that is
running ?'

'Pray step in,' said I. 'You are plucky to show
your face to it!'

'Oh, tut!' he cried; 'it is not for a clergyman any
more than for a seaman to be afraid of weather. I
fear there'll be a call for you, Tregarthen. I thought
I would look round—I have finished my sermon for
to-morrow morning.' And thus talking in a dis-
jointed way while he pulled off his topcoat, he entered
the parlour.

After warming himself and exchanging a few
sentences with my mother about the weather, he began
to talk about the barque.

'Hark to that, now!' he cried, as the wind struck
the front of the house with a crash that had something
of the weight of a great sea in the sound of it, while
you heard it in a roar of thunder overhead, charged
always with an echo of pouring waters; 'what chain
cables wrought by mortal skill are going to hold a
vessel in the eye of all this?'

'What business have they to come here?' cried my
mother.

'I met young Beckerley just now,' continued Mr.
Trembath, 'and he tells me that there's some talk

among our men of there having been a mutiny aboard that Dane.'

'Nothing was said to me about that,' I said.

'Beckerley was in the boat's crew that boarded her,' he went on. 'Probably he imagined a mutiny—misinterpreted a gloomy look among the Danes into an air of revolt. Any way, nothing short of a mutiny should justify a master in anchoring in such a road-stead as this, in the face of the ugliest sky I ever saw in my life.'

'They told me the master was below, ill and helpless,' said I.

He went to the window and parted the curtains to peer through, but the wet ran down the glass, and it was like straining the gaze against a wall of ebony.

'You see,' he continued, coming back to his chair, 'the vessel has those deadly rocks right under her stern, and even if her cables don't part, it is impossible to suppose that she will not drag and be on to them in the blackness, perhaps without her people guessing at their neighbourhood until she touches— and then, God help them !'

'I suppose Pentreath,' exclaimed my mother, naming the second coxswain of the lifeboat, 'is keeping
a look-out?'

'We need not doubt it,' I answered. 'As to her
dragging,' said I, addressing Mr. Trembath, 'the
Danes are as good sailors as the English, and understand their business ; and, mutiny or no mutiny, those
fellows down there are not going to take whatever
may come without a shrewd guess at it, and outcry
enough when it happens. They'll know fast enough
if their vessel is dragging ; then a flare will follow,
and out we shall have to go, of course.'

'We !' said he significantly, looking from me to
my mother. 'You'll not venture to-night, I hope,
Tregarthen.'

'If the call comes, most certainly I shall,' said I,
flushing up, but without venturing to send a glance at
my mother. 'I have appointed myself captain of my
men, and is it for *me*, of all my boat's crew, to shirk
my duty in an hour of extremity ? Let such a thing
happen, and I vow to Heaven I could not show my
face in Tintrenale again.'

Mr. Trembath seemed a little abashed.

'I respect and admire your theory of dutifulness,' said he; 'but you are not an old hand—you are no seasoned boatman in the sense I have in my mind when I think of others of your crew. Listen to this wind! It blows a hurricane, Hugh,' he exclaimed gently; 'you may have the heart of a lion, but have you the skill—the experience——' He halted, looking at my mother.

'If the call comes I will go,' said I, feeling that he reasoned only for my mother's sake, and that in secret his sympathies were with me.

'If the call comes, Hugh must go,' said my mother. 'God will shield him. He looks down upon no nobler work done in this world, none that can better merit His blessing and His countenance.'

Mr. Trembath bowed his head in a heartfelt gesture.

'Yet I hope no call will be made,' she went on. 'I am a mother——' her voice faltered, but she rallied, and said with courage and strength and dignity: 'Yes, I am Hugh's mother. I know what to expect from him, and that whatever his duty may be, he will do it.' Yet in saying this she pressed both her hands to her heart, as though the mere utterance of the words came near to breaking it.

I stepped to her side and kissed her. ' But the call has not yet come, mother,' said I. ' The vessel's anchors may hold bravely, and then, again, the long dark warning of the day will have kept the coast clear of ships.'

To this she made no reply, and I resumed my seat, gladdened to the very heart by her willingness that I should go if a summons came, albeit extorted from her love by perception of my duty ; for had she been reluctant, had she refused her consent indeed, it must have been all the same. I should go whether or not, but in that case with a heavy heart, with a feeling of rebellion against her wishes that would have taken a deal of spirit out of me, and mingled a sense of disobedience with what I knew to be my duty and good in the sight of God and man.

I saw that it comforted my mother to have Mr. Trembath with her, and when he offered to go I begged him to stop and sup with us, and he consented. It was not a time when conversation would flow very easily. The noise of the gale alone was subduing enough, and to this was to be added the restlessness of expectation, the conviction in my own heart that sooner or later the call must come ; and every moment that I talked—putting on as cheerful a face as I could assume—I was waiting for it. I constantly went to the window to look out, guessing that if they burnt a flare aboard the barque the torch-like flame of it would show through the weeping glass ; and shortly before supper was served—that is to say, within a few minutes of nine o'clock—I left the parlour, and going to a room at the extremity of the passage, where I kept my sea-going clothes, I pulled on a pair of stout fisherman's stockings, and over them the sea-boots I always wore when I went in the lifeboat. I then brought away my monkey-jacket and oilskins and sou'wester, and hung them in the passage ready to snatch at ; for a summons to man the boat always meant hurry— there was no time for hunting ; indeed, if the call found the men in bed, their custom was to dress as they ran.

Thus prepared, I returned to the parlour. Mr. Trembath ran his eye over me, but my mother apparently took no notice. A cheerful fire blazed in the grate. The table was hospitable with damask and crystal; the play of the flames set the shadows dancing upon the ceiling that lay in the gloom of the shade over the lamp. There was something in the figure of my old mother, with her white hair and black silk gown and antique gold chain about her neck, that wonderfully fitted that homely interior, warm with the hues of the coal-fire, and cheerful with pictures and with several curiosities of shield and spear, of stuffed bird and Chinese ivory ornament, gathered together by my father in the course of many voyages.

Mr. Trembath looked a plump and rosy and comfortable man as he took his seat at the table, yet there was an expression of sympathetic anxiety upon his face, and frequently I would catch him quietly hearkening, and then he would turn involuntarily to the curtained window, so that it was easy to see in what direction his thoughts went.

'One had need to build strongly in this part of the country,' said he, as we exchanged glances at the sound of a sudden driving roar of wind—a squall of wet of almost hurricane power—to which the im-

mensely strong fabric of our house trembled as though
a heavy battery of cannon were being dragged along
the open road opposite, 'for, upon my word, Hugh,'
said he—we were old friends, and he would as often
as not give me my Christian name—'if the Dane
hasn't begun to drag as yet, there should be good
hope of her holding on throughout what may still be
coming. Surely, for two hours now past her ground-
tackle must have been very heavily tested.'

'My prayer is,' said I, 'that the wind may chop
round and blow off shore. They'll have the sense to
slip then, I hope, and make for the safety of wide
waters, with an amidship helm.'

' He is his father's son,' said Mr. Trembath, smiling
at my mother. 'An amidship helm ! It is as a sailor
would put it. You should have been a sailor, Tregarthen.'

My mother gently shook her head, and then for
some while we ate in silence, the three of us feigning
to look as though we thought of anything else rather
than of the storm that was raging without, and of
the barque labouring to her cables in the black heart
of it.

On a sudden Mr. Trembath let fall his knife and fork. ,

'Hist!' he cried, half rising from his chair.

'The lifeboat bell!' I shouted, catching a note or two of the summons that came swinging along with the wind.

'Oh, Hugh!' shrieked my mother, clasping her hands.

'God keep your dear heart up!' I cried.

I sprang to her side and kissed her, wrung the out-stretched hand of Mr. Trembath, and in a minute was plunging into my peacoat and oilskins. The instant I was out of the house I could hear the fast— I may say the furious—tolling of the lifeboat bell, and sending one glance at the bay, though I seemed almost blinded, and in a manner dazed by the sudden rage of the gale and its burthen of spray and rain against my face, I could distinguish the wavering, flickering yellow light of a flare-up down away in that part of the waters where the Twins and the Deadlow Rock would be terribly close at hand. But I allowed myself no time to look, beyond this hasty glance. Mr. Trembath helped me, by thrusting, to

4—2

pull the house-door after me, for of my own strength
I never could have done it; and then I took to my
heels and drove as best I might headlong through
the living wall of wind, scarcely able to fetch a
breath, reeling to the terrific outflies, yet staggering on.

The gas-flames in the few lamps along the sea-
front were wildly dancing, their glazed frames rattled
furiously, and I remember noticing, even in that
moment of excitement, that one of the lamp-posts
which stood a few yards away from our house had
been arched by the wind as though it were a curve
of leaden pipe. The two or three shops which faced
the sea had their shutters up to save the windows, and
the blackness of the night seemed to be rather heightened than diminished by the dim and leaping glares
of the street lights. But as I neared the lifeboat
house my vision was somewhat assisted by the whiteness of the foam boiling in thunder a long space out.
It flung a dim, elusive, ghostly illumination of its own
upon the air. I could see the outline of the boat-house
against it, the shapes of men writhing, as it seemed,
upon the slipway; the figure of the boat herself,

which had already been eased by her own length out of the house ; and I could even discern, by the aid of that wonderful light of froth, that most of or all her crew were already in her, and that they were stepping her mast, which the roof of the house would not suffer her to keep aloft when she was under shelter.

'Here's the cox'n !' shouted a voice.

'All right, men !' I roared, and with that I rushed through the door of the house, and in a bound or two gained the interior of the boat and my station on the after-grating.

CHAPTER III.

NOW had come the moment when I should need the utmost exertion of nerve and coolness my nature was equal to. There was a large globular lamp alight in the little building—its lustre vaguely touched the boat, and helped me to see what was going on and who were present. Nevertheless I shouted :

'Are all hands aboard ?'

'All hands !' came a hurricane response.

'All got your belts on ?' I next cried.

'All !' was the answer—that is to say, all excepting myself, who, having worn a cork-jacket once, vowed never again to embark thus encumbered.

'Are your sails hooked on ready for hoisting ?' I shouted.

'All ready, sir !'

' And your haul-off rope ?'

' All ready, sir !'

' Now then, my lads—look out, all hands !'

There was a moment's pause :

' Let her go !' I roared.

A man stood close under the stern, ready to pass his knife through the lashing which held the chain to the boat.

' Stand by !' he shouted. ' All gone !'

I heard the clank of the chain as it fell, an instant after the boat was in motion—slowly at first, but in a few breaths she had gathered the full way that her own weight and the incline gave her, and rushed down the slipway, but almost noiselessly, so thickly greased was the timber structure, with some hands hoisting the foresail as she sped, and others grimly and motionless facing seawards, ready to grasp and drag upon the haul-off rope the moment the craft should be water-borne amid the smothering surf.

The thunderous slatting of the sail as the yard mounted, flinging a noise of rending upon the ear as though the cloths were whipping the hurricane in rags, the furious roaring and seething and crackling

and hissing of the mountainous breakers toward
which the boat was darting—the indescribable yelling of the gale sweeping past our ears as the fabric
fled down the ways—the instant sight of the torn and
mangled skies, which seemed dimly revealed somehow
by the snowstorms of froth coursing along the bay—
all this combined into an impression which, though it
could not have taken longer than a second or two to
produce it, dwells upon my mind with so much sharpness that the whole experience of my life might well
have gone to the manufacture of it.

We touched the wash of the sea, and burst through
a cloud of foam ; in the beat of a heart the boat was
up to our knees in water ; in another she was freeing
herself and leaping to the height of the next boiling
acclivity, with my eight men, rigid as iron statues in
their manner of hauling and in their confrontment of
the sea, dragging the craft through the surf and
into deep water by the haul-off rope attached to an
anchor some considerable distance ahead of the end
of the slipway.

At the moment of the boat smiting the first of the
breakers I grasped the tiller-ropes, and on the men

letting go the haul-off line I headed the craft away on the port tack, my intention being to 'reach' down in the direction of Hurricane Point, so as to be able to fetch the barque on a second board.

One had hardly the wits to notice the scene at the first going off, so headlong was the tumble upon the beach, so clamorous the rush of the tempest, and so frightfully wild the leapings and launchings of the boat amid the heavily broken surface of froth. But now she had the weight of the gale in the close-reefed lug that had been shown to it, and this steadied her; and high as the sea ran, yet as the water deepened the surge grew regular, and I was able to settle down to my job of handling the boat, the worst being over, at least so far as our outward excursion went.

I glanced shorewards and observed the blaze of a portfire, held out by a man near the boat-house to serve as a signal to the barque that help was going to her. The fire was blue, the blaze of it was brilliant, and it lighted up a wide area of the foreshore, throwing out the figures of the crowd who watched us, and the outline of the boat-house, and flinging a ghastly tint upon every tall upheaval of surf. The radiance lay in a sort of circle upon the ebony of the night, with what I have named showing in it, as though it was a picture cast by a magic-lantern upon a black curtain. You could see nothing of the lights of the town for it. On either hand of this luminous frame the houses went blending into the land, and each way all was sheer ink.

Shortly after this signal of portfire they sent up a rocket from the barque. It was a crimson ball, and it broke like a flash of lighting under the ragged rush of the sky, and then outleaped afresh the flames of a flare, or, as you might call it, a bonfire, from the deck of the vessel—a burning tar-barrel, perhaps ; and the light of it disclosed the vision of the ship plunging awfully, again and again veiled by storms of crystal which the fathom-high flames of the flare flashed into prisms.

One of our men roared out with an oath : ' She'll have taken the Twins afore we get to her !' and another bellowed : ' Why did they wait to drag a mile afore they signalled ?' But no more was said just then.

Indeed, a man needed to exert the whole strength of his lungs to make himself heard. The edge of the wind seemed to clip the loudest shout as it left the lips, as you would sever a rope with a knife.

Our boat was small for a craft of her character, but a noble, brave, nimble fabric, as had been again and again proved ; and every man of us, allowing that good usage was given her, had such confidence in the *Janet*, that we would not have exchanged her for the largest, handsomest, and best-tested boat on the coast of the United Kingdom. You would have understood her merits had you been with us on this night. I was at the yoke-lines ; Pentreath, my second in command, sat with his foot against the side, gripping the fore-sheet, ready to let go in an instant ; the mizzen had been hoisted, and the rest of the men, crouching down upon the thwarts, sat staring ahead, with iron countenances, with never so much as a stoop among them to the hardest wash of the surge that might sweep with a wild hissing shriek athwart their sea-helmets and half fill the boat as it came bursting in smoke over the weather-bow, till, for the space of a

wink or two, the black gale was as white as a snowstorm overhead.

As we ' reached ' out the sea grew weightier. Never
before had I known a greater sea in that bay. The
ridges seemed to stand up to twice the height of our
masts ; every peak boiled, and as we rose to the
summit of it, the boat was smothered in the foam
of her own churning, and in the headlong, giddy,
dazzling rush into which she soared, with the whole
weight of the gale in her fragment of lug bowing her
over and sending her, as you might have believed, gunwale under down the long, indigo slant of the under-
running billow.

We held on, all as mute as death in the boat.
From time to time as we rose to the head of a sea I
would take a look in the direction of the barque, and
catch a glimpse of the windy spark of her flare, or of
the meteoric sailing of a rocket over her mastheads.
There should have been a moon, but the planet was
without power to strike the faintest illumination into
the heaps and rags of vapours which were pouring up
like smoke over the edge of the raging Atlantic horizon. The picture of the parlour I had just left would

sometimes arise before me : I figured my mother
peering out at the black and throbbing scene of bay ;
I imagined good Mr. Trembath at her side, uttering
such words of comfort and of hope as occurred to
him ; but such fancies as these seemed to be beaten
away by the breath of the hurricane, as rapidly as
they were formed. Should we be in time? If the
vessel's cables parted she was doomed. Nay ; if she
should continue to drag another quarter of an hour,
she would be on to the Twins, and go to pieces as a
child's house of bricks falls to the touch of a hand !

' Ready about !' I roared.

The helm was put down, the fore-sheet eased off,
and round came the boat nobly on the very pinnacle
of a surge, pausing a moment as she was there poised,
and then plunging into the hollow to rise again with
her foresail full, and heading some points to windward
of the vessel we were now steering for.

Through it we stormed, sea after sea bursting from
the lifeboat's bow in pallid clouds which the wind sent
whirling in shrieks—so articulate was the sound of the
slinging spray—into the blackness landwards. Here
and there a tiny spark of lamp flickering in the thick

of the gloom told us the situation of Tintrenale ; but there was nothing more to be seen that way ; the land and the sky above it met in a deep, impenetrable dye, towards which, to leeward of us, the tall seas went flashing in long yearning coils, throbbing into mere pallidness when a cable's length distant.

They had kindled another flare aboard the barque, or else had plied the old one with fresh fuel : she was visible by the light of the flames, the white of her furled canvas coming and going to the fluctuating fires ; and I marked, with a heart that sank in me, the dreadful manner of her labouring. She was pitching bows under, and rolling too, and by the shining of the signal-fire upon her deck offered a most wonderful sight, rendered terrible also by a view that we could now get of a crowd of men hanging in a lump in her starboard fore-rigging.

The second coxswain flashed a portfire that they might know the lifeboat was at hand, and we went plunging and sweeping down to a point some little distance ahead of the barque, the crowd of us irradiated by the stream of emerald-green flame.

' All ready with the anchor, lads ?' I shouted.

' All ready, sir !' was the answer.

' Down foresail !' and as I gave this order I put the helm down and brought the boathead to wind about thirty fathoms ahead of the ship.

' Let go the anchor !'

' Unstep the foremast !' bawled the second coxswain, and, while this was doing, he and another swiftly lifted the mizzen-mast out of its bearings and laid it along.

' Veer away cable handsomely !' I shouted ; and pitching and foaming, now dropping into a hollow that seemed fifty feet deep, now appearing to scale a surge that lifted the boat's bow almost dead on end over her stern—all in a fashion to make the brain of the stoutest and most experienced among us reel again —we dropped alongside.

In what followed there was so much confusion, so much uproar, such distraction of shouts in foreign and unintelligible accents, such a terrible washing of seas, such bewilderment born of the darkness, of the complicated demands upon the attention through need of keeping the boat clear of the huge chopping bows of the barque, through bawling to the men in the rigging and receiving answers which we could not understand, that this passage of my singular adventure could scarcely be less vague to me in memory if, instead of having been an actor in it, I had read it in a book.

There were six or seven men, as well as I could make out, clustered in the fore-rigging. I believed I could see others in the mizzen-shrouds. This being my notion, my consuming anxiety was to drop the boat down on the quarter as quickly as possible, for it was not only that the Twins were within a cable's range astern, with the fury of the foam there making a kind of shining upon the water that might have passed for moonlight : such was the volume and height of the sea roaring betwixt the labouring ship and our boat, that at every toss of the little fabric, at every ponderous lean down of the great groaning black hull towering over us, we stood to be staved.

The fellows in the fore-rigging seemed to be stupefied. We all of us yelled, ' Jump, jump ! Watch as she rises, and jump for God's sake !' meanwhile keeping a turn of the cable so as to hold the boat abreast of them. It seemed an eternity before they understood, and yet a minute had not passed since we dropped down, when a cry broke from them, and first one jumped, and then another, and then the rest of them sprang, and there they were lying in a huddle in the bottom of the boat, one or two of them groaning dreadfully, as though from broken limbs, or worse injuries still, all of them motionless as they lay when they jumped, like folk nearly dead of terror and cold and pain.

'Veer out now, my lads! veer out!' I cried; 'handsomely, that we may get smartly under the mizzen-shrouds.'

'There's nobody there, sir,' roared one of my men.

No! I looked and found it had been an illusion of my sight, due to the flame of the flare that was burning fiercely on the main-deck.

'Are you all here?' I cried, addressing the dusky huddle of men at the bottom of the boat.

Something was said, but the gale deafened me, and I could catch no meaning, no syllables indeed, in the answer.

'They'll all be here, sir,' shouted one of my crew; 'the port-davits are empty, and some'll have left in the boat.'

A great sea swung us up at that instant flush with

the level of the bulwark-rails, with a heel of the barque that disclosed her decks bare to the bright fires of the signal.

'They must be all here!' I cried; 'but look well. Is there one among you who can catch any signs of a living man on board?'

They waited for the next upheaval of sea; then rose a shout: 'They're all here, sir, you'll find.'

'Heave ahead then, my lads!' by which I meant that they should haul upon the cable to drag the boat clear of the dreadful crushing, shearing chop of the overhanging bows of the barque.

At that instant a head showed over the rail a little abaft the fore-shrouds, and the clear, piercing voice of a boy cried, with as good an English accent as I myself have, 'My father is ill and helpless in the cabin. Do not leave us!'

'No, no, we'll not leave you,' I instantly shouted in return, sending my voice fair to the lad from the height of a sea that· pretty well brought his and my head on a level. 'How many are there of you?'

'Two,' was the answer.

I had to wait for the boat to slide up to the summit

of the next surge ere I could call out again. The black yawns betwixt us and the barque might have passed for valleys looked at from a hillside, so horribly hollow and deep were they; they were pale and yet dusky too, with sheets of foam; a soul-confounding noise of thunderous washing and seething rose up from them. When we were in one of those hollows the great mass of the dark fabric of the barque seemed to tower fifty feet above us, and we lay becalmed, hanging, while you might have counted five, in absolute stagnation, with the yell of the wind sweeping over our heads as though we were in the heart of a pit.

'Cannot your father help himself *at all?*' I bawled to the boy.

'He cannot stir; he must be lifted!' he answered in a shriek, for his high, clear, piercing cry thus sounded.

'By Heaven, then, lads,' I bawled to my men, 'there's no time to be lost! We must bundle the poor fellow over somehow, and help the lad. Nothing will have been done if we leave them behind us. Watch your chance and follow me, three of you!'

At the instant of saying this I made a spring from off the height of the gratings on which I stood, and got into the fore-chains, the boat then being on the level of that platform ; and as actively as a cat, for few young fellows had nimbler limbs, I scrambled over the bulwark on to the deck, just in time to escape a huge fold of rushing water that foamed sheer through the chains with a spite and weight that must instantly have settled my business for me.

I was in the act of running along the deck to where the lad stood—that is to say, a little forward of the gangway, not doubting that the others of my crew whom I had called upon were following with as much alertness as I had exhibited, when I felt a shock as of a thump pass through the barque.

' She has struck !' thought I.

But hardly was I sensible of this tremor through the vessel, when there arose a wild and dreadful cry from alongside—heavenly God ! how am I to describe that shocking noise of human distress ?   I fled to the rail and looked over ; it was all boiling water under me, with just a sight of the black line of the gunwale or of the keel of the lifeboat ; but there was such a raging

of foam, such a thickness of seething yeast smoking
into the hurricane as though some volcanic eruption
had happened right under the barque, filling the air
with steam, that there was nothing whatever to be
seen saving just that dark glance of keel or gunwale,
as I have said, which, however, vanished as I looked in
the depth of the hissing spumy smother. I knew by
this that the lifeboat must have been staved and filled
by a sudden fling of her against the massive sides of
the barque; for she was a self-righting craft, and,
though she might have thrown every soul in her out
as she rolled over, yet she would have rose buoyant
again, emptying herself as she leapt to the surge, and
there she would have been alongside, without a living
creature in her if you will, but a good boat, and riding
stoutly to her cable. But she had been stove, and now
she was gone!

The blazing tar-barrel on the main-deck enabled me
to see my way to rush aft. I cried to the lad as I sped :
' The boat is staved ; all hands of her are overboard and
drowning ! Heave ropes' ends over the side ! fling
life-buoys !' And thus shouting, scarcely knowing,
indeed, what I called out, so confounded was I, so

shocked, so horrified, so heartbroken, I may say, by the suddenness and the fearfulness of this disaster, I reached the quarter of the barque and overhung it; but I could see nothing. The cloudy boiling rose and fell, and with every mighty drop of the great square counter of the barque, the sea swept in a roar from either hand of her with a cataractal fury that would rush whatever was afloat in it dozens of fathoms distant at every *scend.* Here and there *now* I believe I could distinguish some small black object, but the nearer pallid waters dimmed into a blackness at a little distance, and, if those dark points which I observed were the heads of swimmers, then such was the headlong race of the surge they were swept into the throbbing dusk ere I could make sure of them.

I stood as one paralyzed from head to foot. My inability to be of the least service to my poor comrades and the unhappy Danes caused me to feel as though the very heart in me had ceased to beat. The young fellow came to my side.

'What is to be done?' he cried.

'Nothing!' I answered in a passion of grief. 'What can be done? God grant that many of them will reach the shore! The hurl of the sea is landwards, and their life-belts will float them. But your people are doomed.'

'And so are we!' he exclaimed shrilly, yet without perceptible terror, with nothing worse than wild excitement in his accents. 'There are rocks directly under our stern. Are you a sailor?'

'No!'

'O, du gode Gud! what is to be done?' cried the lad.

I cast my eyes despairingly around. The tar-barrel was still burning bravely upon the deck, defying the ceaseless sweeping of spray from over the bows ; the windy unearthly light tinctured the ship with its sickly sallow hue to the height of her lower yards, and the whole ghastly body of her was to be seen as she rolled and plunged under a sky that was the blacker for the light of the distress-flare, and upon a sea whose vast spreads of creaming brows would again and again come charging along to the very height of the bulwark rail.

In the midst of this pause on my part, and while every instinct of self-preservation in me was blindly

flinging itself, so to speak, against the black and
horrible situation that imprisoned me, and while I
was hopelessly endeavouring to consider what was to
be done to save the young fellow alongside of me
from destruction—for, as to his father, it was impossible to extend my sympathies at such a moment
to one whom I had not seen, who did not appeal to
me, as it were, in form and voice for succour—I say,
in the midst of this pause of hopeless deliberation,
the roar of the hurricane ceased on a sudden.
Nothing more, I was sure, was signified by this than
a lull, to be followed by some fierce chop round, or by
the continuance of the westerly tempest with a bitterer
spite in the renewed rush of it. The lull may have
lasted ten or fifteen seconds. In that time I do not
know that there was a breath of air to be felt outside
the violent eddyings and draughts occasioned by the
sickening motions of the barque. I looked up at the
sky, and spied the leanest phantom of a star that
glimmered for the space of a single swing of a pen-
dulum, and then vanished behind a rushing roll of
vapour of a midnight hue, winging with incredible
velocity *from* the land.

So insupportable was the movement of the deck that I was forced to support myself by a belaying-pin, or I must have been thrown. My companion clung to a similar pin close beside me. The thunder of running and colliding waters rose into that magical hush of tempest; I could hear the booming of the surf as far as Hurricane Point and the caldron-like noises of the waters round about the rocks astern of us.

'Has the storm ceased?' cried my companion. 'Oh, beloved father, we may be spared yet!' he added, extending his disengaged hand towards the deck-house, as he apostrophized the helpless man who lay there.

Amazed as I was by this instant cessation of the gale, I could yet find mind enough to be struck by my companion's manner, by his words, and now, I may say, by his voice also. I was about to address him; but, as my lips parted, there was a vivid flash of lightning that threw out the whole scene of bay, cliff, foreshore, and town, with the line of the horizon seawards, in a dazzle of violet; a crash of thunder followed; but, before its ear-splitting reverberation had ceased, the echoes of it were drowned in the bellowing of the gale coming directly off the land.

What is there in words to express the fury of this outfly? It met the heave of the landward-running seas, and swept them into smoke, and the air grew as white and thick with spume as though a heavy snowstorm were blowing horizontally along. It took the barque and swung her; her labouring was so prodigious as she was thrust by this fresh hurricane broadside round to the surge, that I imagined every second she would founder under my feet. I felt a shock : my companion cried, 'One of the cables has parted!' A moment later I felt the same indescribable tremble running through the planks on which we stood.

'Is that the other cable gone, do you think?' I shouted.

'There is a lead-line over the side,' he cried ; 'it will tell us if we are adrift.'

I followed him to near the mizzen rigging ; neither of us durst let go with one hand until we had a grip of something else with the other ; it was *now* not only the weight of the wind that would have laid us prone and pinned us to the deck—a pyramidal sea had sprung up as though by enchantment, and each apex as it soared about the bows and sides was blown inboards in very avalanches of water, which with each violent roll of the vessel poured in a solid body to the rail, one side or the other, again and again, to the height of our waist.

My companion extended his hand over the bulwarks, and cried out : ' Here is the lead-line. It stretches towards the bows. Oh, sir, we are adrift ! we are blowing out to sea !'

I put my hand over and grasped the line, and instantly knew by the angle of it that the lad was right. By no other means would he have been able to get at the truth. The weight of lead, by resting on the bottom, immediately told if the barque was dragging. All around was white water ; the blackness of the night drooped to the very spit of the brine ; not a light was to be perceived, not the vaguest outline of the cliff ; and the whole scene of darkness was the more bewildering for the throb of the near yeast upon the eyesight.

' Is your binnacle-light burning ?' I cried.

The lad answered, 'Yes.'

'Then,' I shouted, 'we must find out the quarter the gale has shifted into and get her stern on to it, and clear Hurricane Point, if Almighty God will permit. There may be safety in the open ; there is none here.'

With the utmost labour and distress we made our way aft. The flare had been extinguished by the heavy falls of water, and it was worse than walking blindfolded. The binnacle-light was burning—this was, indeed, to be expected. The barque was plunging directly head to wind, and a glance at the card enabled me to know that the gale was blowing almost due east, having shifted, as these cyclonic ragings often do, right into the quarter opposite whence it had come.

'We must endeavour to get her before it,' I cried ; 'but I am no sailor. There may come another shift, and we ought to clear the land while the hurricane holds as it does. What is to be done ?'

'Will she pay off if the helm is put hard over ?' he answered. 'Let us try it !'

He seized the spokes on one side ; I put my shoulder

to the wheel on the other, and thus we jammed and
secured the helm into the posture called by sailors
'hard a-starboard.' She fell off, indeed—into the
trough, and there she lay, amid such a diabolical
play of water, such lashings of seas on both sides, as
it is not in mortal pen to portray !

Had we been in the open ocean, a better attitude
than the barque herself had taken up we could not
have wished for. She was, indeed, 'hove-to,' as the
sea-expression is, giving something of her bow to the
wind, and was in that posture which the ship-master
will put his vessel into in such a tempest as was now
blowing. But, unhappily, the land was on either hand
of us, and though our drift might be straight out to
sea, I could not be sure that it was. The tide would
be making to the west and north ; the coils and pyra-
mids and leapings of surge had also a sort of yearning and leaning towards north-west, as if in sympathy
with the tide ; the deadly terrace of Hurricane Point
lay that way ; and so the leaving of the barque in the
trough of the sea might come, indeed, to cost us our
lives, which had only just been spared by the shift in
the storm of wind.

'She does not answer the helm,' I cried to my young companion.

'Her head will pay off,' he answered, 'if we can manage to hoist a fragment of sail forward. It *must* be done, sir. Will you help me?'

'God knows I will do anything!' I cried. 'Show me what is to be done. We must save our lives if we can. There may be a chance out on the ocean for us.'

Without another word he went forward, and I followed him. We had to pause often to preserve ourselves from being floated off our feet. The flood, which washed white betwixt the rails, lifted the rigging off the pins, and sent the ropes snaking about the decks, and our movements were as much hampered as though we fought our way through a jungle. The foam all about us, outside and inboards, put a wild, cold glimmer into the air, which enabled us to distinguish outlines. In fact, at moments the whole shape of the barque, from her bulwarks to some distance up her masts, would show like a sketch in ink upon white paper as she leaned off the slant of the sea and painted her figure upon the hill of froth thundering away from her on the lee-side.

My companion paused for a moment or two under the shelter of the caboose or galley, to tell me what he meant to do. We then crawled on to the fore-castle, and he bade me hold by a rope which he put into my hand, and await his return. I watched him creep into the 'eyes' of the vessel and get upon the bowsprit, but after that I lost sight of him, for the seas smoked so fiercely all about the ship's head—to every plunge of her bows there rose so shrouding a thickness of foam—that the air was a fog of crystals where the lad was, and had he gone overboard he could not have vanished more utterly from my sight. Indeed, I could not tell whether he was gone or not, and a feeling of horror possessed me when I thought of being left alone in the vessel with a sick and use-less man lying somewhere aft, and with the rage and darkness of the dreadful storm around me, the chance of striking upon Hurricane Point, and no better hope at the best than what was to be got out of thinking of the midnight breast of the storming Atlantic.

After a few minutes there was the noise of the

rattling of canvas resembling a volley of small shot
fired off the bows. The figure of the lad came from
the bowsprit out of a burst of spray that soared in
steam into the wind.

'Only a fragment must be hoisted!' he exclaimed
with his mouth at my ear. 'Pull with me!'

I put my weight upon the rope, and together we
rose a few feet of the sail upon the stay—it was the
foretopmast staysail, as I afterwards discovered.

'Enough!' cried my companion in his clear, penetrating voice; 'if it will but hold till the vessel pays
off, all will be well. We dare not ask for more.'

He secured the rope we had dragged upon to a pin,
and I followed him aft, finding leisure even in that
time of distress and horror to wonder at the coolness,
the intrepidity of soul, that was expressed in his clear
unfaltering speech, in the keen judgment and instant
resolution of a lad whose age, as I might gather from
his voice, could scarcely exceed fifteen or sixteen
years. Between us we seized the wheel afresh, one
on either side of it, and waited. But we were not to
be kept long in suspense. Indeed, even before we
had grasped the helm, the barque was paying off.

The rag of canvas held nobly, and to the impulse of it the big bows of the vessel rounded away from the gale, and in a few minutes she was dead before it, pitching furiously, with the sea snapping and foaming to her taffrail and quarters.

But the thickness of her yards, with the canvas rolled up on them, the thickness of the masts, too, the spread of the tops, the complicated gear of shroud, backstay, and running rigging—all offered resistance enough to the dark and living gale that was bellowing right over the stern to put something of the speed of an arrow into the keel of the fabric. Through it she madly raced, with pallid clouds blowing about her bows, and white peaks hissing along her sides, and a wake of snow under her counter heaving to half the height of the mizzenmast with the hurl of the seas, and a ceaseless blowing of froth over our heads as the lad and I stood together grasping the wheel, steering the vessel into the darkness of the great Atlantic Ocean, with our eyes upon the compass-card, whose illuminated disc showed the course on which we were being flashed forwards by the storm to be a trifle south of west.

CHAPTER IV.

HELGA NIELSEN.

FOR full twenty minutes the lad and I clung to the helm without exchanging a word. The speed of the driven vessel rendered her motion comparatively easy, after the intolerable lurching and rolling and plunging of her as she lay at anchor or in the trough. She was swept onwards with such velocity that I had little or no fear of her taking in the seas over her stern, and she steered well, with but little wildness in the swerving of her bows, as was to be seen by the comparative regularity of the oscillation of the compass-card.

This running before the tempest, of course, diminished the volume and power of it, so far, I mean, as our own sensations were concerned ; but the sight of the sea, as much of it at least as was visible, coupled with the thunder of the wind up aloft in the sky, and the prodigious crying and shrieking and shrilling of it in the rigging, was warrant enough that were we to heave the barque to we should find the hurricane harder now than it had been at any other time since it first came on to blow. Yet our racing before it, as I have said, seemed somewhat to lull it, and we could converse without having to cry out, though for twenty minutes we stood mute as statues waiting and watching.

At last my companion said to me: 'Have we passed that point which you spoke of, do you think?'

'Oh yes,' I answered. 'It would not be above two miles distant from the point where we broke adrift. Our speed cannot have been less than eight or nine knots. I should say Hurricane Point is a full mile away down on the quarter there.'

'I fear that we shall find the sea,' said he, 'grow terribly heavy as we advance.'

'Yes,' said I; 'but what is to be done? There is nothing for it but to advance. Suppose such another shift of wind as has just happened—what then? We should have a line of deadly shore right under our lee. No, we must hold on as we are.'

'There are but two of us!' cried he : 'my father cannot count. What are we to do? We cannot work this big ship!'

'The weather may break,' said I ; 'it is surely too fierce ˜to last. What can we hope for but to be rescued or assisted by some passing vessel ? Is this ship stanch ?'

'Yes ; she is a strong ship,' he replied. 'She is about six years old. My father is her owner. I wish I could go to him,' he added ; 'he will be dying to learn what has happened and what is being done, and it is past the time for his medicine, and he will be wanting his supper!'

I tried to catch a view of him as he spoke these words, but the haze of the binnacle-lamp did not reach to his face, and it was as black as the face of the sky itself out of that sheen. What he had said had a girlish note in it that I could not reconcile with his dress, with his seafaring alertness, with his spirited behaviour, his nimble crawling out upon the bowsprit, and his perception of what was to be done, under conditions which might well have clouded the wits of the oldest and most audacious sailor.

'Pray go and see your father,' said I. 'I believe I can keep this helm amidships without help.' And, indeed, if I could not have steered the barque alone, I do not know that such assistance as he could offer would have suffered me to control her. He seemed but a slender lad—so far, at least, as I had been able to judge from the view I got when the flare was burn-ing—very quick, but without such strength as I should have looked for in a young seaman, as I could tell whenever the wheel had to be put up or down.

He let go the spokes, and stood apart for a minute or two, as though to judge whether I could manage without him ; then said he, 'I will return quickly,' and with that he took a step and vanished in the blackness forward of the binnacle-stand.

My mind dwelt for a moment upon him, upon the clearness and purity of his voice, upon a something in his speech which I could not define, and which puzzled me; upon his words, which were as good English as one could hope to hear at home, albeit there was a certain sharpness and incisiveness—per-haps I might say a little of harshness—in his accent-uation that might suggest him a foreigner to an

English ear, though, as I then supposed, it was more likely than not this quality arose from the excitement and dismay and distress which worked in him as in me.

But he speedily ceased to engage my thoughts. What could I dwell upon but the situation in which I found myself—the spectacle of the black outline of barque painting herself upon the volumes of white water she hove up around her as she rushed forward pitching bows under, her rigging echoing with unearthly cries, as if the dark waving mass of spar and gear aloft were crowded with tormented souls wailing and howling and shrieking dismally ?   I recalled my mother's dream ; I believed I was acting in some dreadful nightmare of my own slumbers ; all had happened so suddenly—so much of emotion, of wild excitement, of agitation, and, I may say, horror, had been packed into the slender space of time between the capsizal of the lifeboat and this rushing out of the bay, that, now I had a little leisure to bend my mind to contemplation of the reality, I could not believe in it as an actual thing.   I was dazed ; my hearing was stunned by the ceaseless roar of wind

and seas. The *Janet* stove and sunk! All my lion-
hearted men drowned, perhaps! The poor Danes, for
whom they had forfeited their lives, long ago corpses!
Would not this break my mother's heart? Would
there be a survivor to tell her that when I was last
seen I was aboard the barque? Once again I figured
the little parlour I had quitted but a few hours since
—I pictured my mother sitting by the fire, waiting
and listening—the long night, the bitter anguish of
suspense!—it was lucky for me that the obligation of
having to watch and steer the vessel served as a constant intrusion upon my mind at this time, for could
I have been able to sit down and surrender myself
wholly to my mood, God best knows how it must
have gone with me.

The lad was about ten minutes absent. I found
him alongside the wheel without having witnessed
his approach. He came out of the darkness as a
spirit might shape itself, and I did not know that
he was near me until he spoke.

' My father says that our safety lies in heading into
the open sea, to obtain what you call a wide offing,'
said he.

' What does he advise ?' I asked.

' " We must continue to run," he says,' answered the lad, meaning by *run* that we should keep the barque before the wind. ' " When the coast is far astern we must endeavour to heave to." So he counsels. I told him we are but two. He answered, " It may be done." '

' I wish he were able to leave his cabin and take charge,' said I. ' What is his complaint ?'

' He was seized, shortly after leaving Cuxhaven, with rheumatism in the knees,' he answered ; ' he cannot stand—cannot, indeed, stir either leg.'

' Why did he not get himself conveyed ashore for treatment ?'

' He hoped to get better. We were to call at Swansea before proceeding to Porto Allegre, and if he had found himself still ill when he arrived there, it was his intention to procure another captain for the *Anine*, and remain at Swansea with me until he was able to return home.'

' Who had charge of the barque when she brought up in the bay ?' I inquired, finding a sort of relief in asking these questions, and, indeed, in having some-

body to converse with, for even my ten minutes of
loneliness at the helm of that pitching and foaming
vessel had depressed me to the very core of my
soul.

‘ The carpenter, who acted as second mate.’

‘ Yes, I recollect some of our boatmen brought the
news. Your chief mate broke his leg and was sent
ashore. But did your father consent to the *Anine*
dropping anchor in so perilous a bay as ours—
perilous, I mean, considering the weather at the
time ?’

‘ He was at the mercy of the man Damm—the
carpenter, I mean,’ he answered. ‘ The crew had
refused to keep the sea : they said a tempest was
coming, and that shelter must be sought before the
wind came, and the carpenter steered the barque for
the first haven he fell in with, which happened to be
your bay. Our crew were not good men ; they were
grumbling much, as your English word is, from the
hour of our leaving Cuxhaven.’

‘ But surely,’ said I, ‘ the poor fellows who sprang
out of the fore-rigging could not have formed the
whole of the crew of a ship of this burthen.’

'No,' he answered ; 'the carpenter and five men got away in one of the boats when they found that the barque was dragging her anchors. They lowered one boat, which filled and was knocked to pieces, and the wreck of it, I dare say, is still swinging at the tackles. They lowered the other boat and went away in her.'

' Did they reach the shore ?'

' I do not know,' said he.

' They must have been a bad lot,' said I—' those who escaped in the boat and those who hung in the shrouds, to leave your helpless father to his fate.'

' Oh ! a bad lot, a wicked lot !' he cried. ' They were not Danes,' he added. ' Danish sailors would not have acted as those men did.'

' Are you a Dane?' I asked.

' My father is,' he answered. ' I am as much English as Danish. My mother was an English-woman.'

' I should have believed you wholly English,' said I. ' Are you a sailor ?'

He answered, ' No.' I was about to speak, when he exclaimed : ' I am a girl !'

Secretly for some time I had supposed this, and yet I was hardly less astonished than had I been without previous suspicion.

'A *girl!*' I cried, sending my sight groping over her figure ; but to no purpose. She was absolutely indistinguishable saving her arms, which were dimly touched by the haze of the binnacle-light as they lay upon the spokes of the wheel.

'It is my whim to dress as a boy on board ship !' she exclaimed, with no stammer of embarrassment that I could catch in her clear delivery, that penetrated to my ear without loss of a syllable through the heavy storming of the gale, flashing with the fury of a whirlwind off the brows of the seas which rushed at us, as the barque's counter soared into the whole weight and eye of the tempest.

So far had we conversed ; but at this moment a great surge took the barque and swung her up in so long, so dizzy, and sickening an upheaval, followed by so wild a fall into the frothing hollow at its base, that speech was silenced in me, and I could think of nothing else but the mountainous billows now running. Indeed, as my companion had predicted, the farther we drew out from the land the heavier we found the sea. The play of the ocean, indeed, out here, was rendered fierce beyond words by the dual character of the tempest ; for the seas which had been set racing out of the west had not yet been conquered by the violence of the new gale and by the hurl of the liquid hills out of the east ; and the barque was now labouring in the same sort of pyramidal sea as had run in the bay, saving that here the whole power of the great Atlantic was in each billow, and the fight between the contending waters was as a combat of mighty giants.

The decks were full of water ; at frequent intervals the brow of the sea rushing past us, swift as was our own speed upon its careering back, would arch over the rail and tumble aboard in a heavy fall of water, and the smoke of it would rise from the planks as though the barque were on fire, and make the blackness forward of the mainmast hoary. I sought in vain for the least break in the dark ceiling of the sky. Will the vessel be able to keep afloat ? I was now all the time asking myself. Is it possible for any structure put together by human hands to outlive

such a night of fury as this? As I have said, I was
no sailor, yet my 'longshore training gave me very
readily to know that the best, if not the only, chance
for our lives was to get the barque hove-to, and leave
her to breast the seas and live the weather out as she
could with her helm lashed, and, perhaps some bit
of tarpaulin in the weather-rigging, to keep her head
up. But this, that was to be easily wished, was inexpressibly perilous to attempt or achieve, for, in
bringing the vessel to, it was as likely as not we
should founder out of hand. A single sea might be
enough to do our business ; and, failing that, there was
the almost certain prospect of the decks being swept,
of every erection from the taffrail to the bows being
carried away, ourselves included ; of a score of leaks
being started by a single blow, and, even if the girl
and I managed to hold on, of the barque foundering
under our feet.

Thus we rushed onward, very literally indeed scudding under bare poles, as it is called ; and for a long
while we had neither of us a word to exchange, so
present was calamity, so near was death, so dreadful
were the thunderous sounds of the night, so engross-

ing our business of keeping the flying fabric dead before the seas.

I pulled out my watch and held it hastily to the binnacle-lamp, and found the hour exactly one. The girl asked me the time. This was the first word that had passed between us for a long while. I replied, and she said in a voice that indicated extraordinary spirit, but that nevertheless sounded languishingly after her earlier utterance : ' Now that it is past midnight, the gale may break ; surely such fierce weather cannot last for many hours !'

' I wish you would go,' said I, 'and get some refreshment for yourself, and lie down for awhile. I believe I can manage singlehanded to keep the vessel before it.'

' If I lie down, it would not be to sleep,' she answered ; ' but if you think I can be spared from the wheel for a few minutes, I will obtain some refreshment for us both, and I should also like to see how my father does.'

I answered that if the helm was to prove too heavy for me, her help might hardly save me from being obliged to let go.

' Do not believe this,' she exclaimed, ' because you now know that I am a girl !'

'I have had no heart to express wonderment as yet,' said I, ' otherwise my astonishment and admiration would reassure you, if you suppose I doubt your strength and capacity now that I know you to be a girl. A little refreshment will help us both,' and I was going to advise her to seize the opportunity to attire herself in dry clothes, for I was in oilskins, whereas, so far as I was able to gather, her dress was a pea-jacket and a cloth cap; and I knew that again and again she had been soaked to the skin, and that the wind pouring on her would be chilling her to her very heart. But even amid such a time as this I was sensible of a diffidence in naming what was in my mind, and held my peace.

She left the wheel, and I stood steering the barque single-handed, with my eyes fixed upon the illuminated compass-card, while I noticed that the course the vessel was taking, which always held her dead before the gale, was now above a point, nay, perhaps two points, to the southward of west, whence it was clear the hurricane was veering northwardly.

Whether it was because this small shift in the wind
still found the colliding seas travelling east and west,
or that some heavy surge sweeping its volume along
the starboard bow caused the barque to ' yaw ' widely,
as it is termed, and so brought a great weight of billow against the rudder : be the cause what it will,
while my eye was rooted upon the card, the stern of
the vessel was on a sudden run up with the velocity
of a balloon from whose car all the ballast has been
thrown, the spokes were wrenched from my hand as
they revolved like the driving-wheel of a locomotive
in full career, and I was sent spinning against the
bulwark, from which I dropped upon my knees and
so rolled over, stunned.

For all I could tell I might have lain five minutes
or five hours without my senses. I believe I was
brought to by the washing over me of the water that
lay in that lee-part of the deck into which I had been
shot. I sat erect, but for a long while was unable to
collect my mind, so bewildered were my brains by the
fall, and so confounded besides by the uproar round
about. I then made out the figure, as I took it, of
the girl standing at the wheel, and got on my legs,

and after feeling over myself, so to speak, to make sure that all my bones were sound, I staggered, or rather clawed my way up to the wheel ; for the barque seemed now to me to be upon her beam-ends, and rolling with dreadful wildness, and there were times when the foaming waters rushed inboards over the rail which she submerged to leeward.

The girl cried out when she spied me. I had to draw close, indeed, to be seen ; it was as black down where I was thrown, as the inside of the vessel's hold. She cried out, I say, uttering some Danish exclamation, and then exclaimed :

'I feared you were lost ; I feared that you had been thrown overboard ; I ought not to have left you alone at the wheel. Tell me if you are hurt ?'

'No ; I am uninjured,' I replied. 'But what has become of the ship ? I am only just recovered from my swoon.'

'Oh !' she cried, 'she has taken up the very situation you wished for. She has hove herself to. She came broadside to the sea after you were flung from the wheel. We are mercifully watched over. We dared not of ourselves have brought her to the wind.'

All my senses were now active in me once more, and I could judge for myself. It was as the girl had said. The barque had fallen into the trough, and had taken up a position for herself, and was shouldering the heavy western surge with her bow, coming to and falling off in rhythmic sweep. Clouds of froth repeatedly broke over her forecastle ; but she seemed while I then watched her to rise buoyant to each black curl of billow as it took her amidships.

' Will you help me to lash the helm ?' cried the girl. ' It is all that the *Anine* will need, I am sure. She will be able to fight the storm alone if we can secure the wheel.'

Between us, we drove the helm ' hard a-lee,' to use the sea term—for which, indeed, it is impossible to find an equivalent, though I trust to be as sparing in this language as the obligation of explanation will permit—and then, by means of ropes wound round the spokes, so bound the wheel as to cripple all play in it.

' Will she lie up to the wind, do you think,' said I, ' without some square of canvas abaft here to keep her head to it ?'

'I have been watching her. I believe she will do very well,' the girl answered. 'I feared that that little head of sail we hoisted in the bay would blow her bows round, and, by this not happening, I suppose that sail is in rags. One would not have heard it split in such a thunder of wind as this.'

'Have you seen your father?'

'Yes. I was talking to him when you were thrown from the wheel. I knew what had happened by the behaviour of the vessel. I ran out, and feared you were lost.'

'What does he counsel?'

'It is still his wish that we should go on putting plenty of sea betwixt us and the land. But do you notice that the gale has gone somewhat into the north? He will be glad to hear it, now that we are no longer scudding. Our drift should put us well clear of the Land's End, and, indeed, I dare say now we are being thrust away at several miles in the hour from the coast. He is very anxious to know if the *Anine* has taken in water, and wishes me to sound the well. I fear I shall not be able to do this alone.'

'Why should you?' cried I. 'You shall do nothing

7—2

alone! I cannot credit that you are a girl! Such
spirit—such courage—such knowledge of a calling
the very last in the wide world that women are likely
to understand! Pray let me ask your name ?'

'Helga Nielsen,' she answered. 'My father is
Peter Nielsen—Captain Peter Nielsen,' she repeated.
'And your name?'

'Hugh Tregarthen,' said I.

'It is sad that you should be here,' said she,
'brought away from your home, suffering all this
hardship and peril! You came to save our lives.
God will bless you, sir. I pray that the good God
may protect and restore you to those you love.'

Spite of the roar of the wind, and the ceaseless
crashing and seething sound of the smiting and colliding seas, I could catch the falter of emotion in her
voice as she pronounced these words ; but then, as
you will suppose, we were close together, standing
shoulder to shoulder against the binnacle, while we
exchanged these sentences.

'There is refreshment in the cabin,' said she, after
a pause of a moment or two. 'You need support.
This has been a severe night of work for you, sir,

from the hour of your putting off to us in the lifeboat.'

I found myself smiling at the motherly tenderness
conveyed in the tone of her voice. I longed to have
a clear view of her, for it was still like talking in a
pitch-dark room ; the binnacle-lamp needed trimming,
its light was feeble, and the sky lay horribly black
over the ocean, that was raging, ghastly with pallid
glances of sheets of foam under it.

' Let us first sound the well, if possible,' said I, ' for
our lives' sake we ought to find out what is happening
below !'

By this time we had watched and waited long
enough to satisfy ourselves that the barque would
do as well as we dared hope with her helm lashed ;
and it also happened, very fortunately, that her
yards were in the right trim for the posture in which
she lay, having been pointed to the wind—the fore-
yards on one tack, the main-yards on the other—when
the gale came on to blow in the bay, and the
braces had not since been touched. I walked with
the girl to the entrance of the deck-house, the door of
which faced forwards. She entered the structure and,

while I waited outside, lighted a bull's-eye lamp, with
which she rejoined me, and together we went forward
to another house built abaft of the galley. This had
been the place in which the crew slept. The carpenter's chest was here, and also the sounding-rod. We
then went to the pumps, and while I held the lamp
she dropped the rod down the sounding-pipe, drew
it up and brought it to the light and examined it, and
named the depth of water there was in the hold. I
do not recollect the figure, but I remember that,
though it was significant, there was nothing greatly to
alarm us in it, seeing how heavily and how frequently
the barque had been flooded with the seas, and how
much of the water might have made its way from
above.

I recount this little passage in a few lines, yet it
forms one of the most sharp-cut of the memories of
my adventure. The picture is before me as I write.
I see the pair of us as we come to a dead stand,
grasping each other for support, while the vessel rolls
madly over on the slope of some huge hurtling sea.
I see the bright glare from the bull's-eye lamp in the
girl's hand, dancing like a will-o'-the-wisp upon the

black flood betwixt the rails washing with the slant
of the decks to our knees; I see her dropping the rod
down the tube, coolly examining it, declaring its indication, while, to the flash of the lamplight, I catch
an instant's glimpse of her face, shining out white—
large-eyed, as it seemed to me—upon the blackness
rushing in thunder athwart the deck.

She led the way into the deck-house. There was a
small lantern wildly swinging at a central beam—my
companion had lighted it when she procured the bull's-
eye lamp—it diffused a good lustre, and I could see
very plainly. It was just a plain, ordinary, shipboard
interior, with three little windows of a side, a short
table, lockers on either hand, and a sleeping-berth, or
cabin, designed for the captain's use, aft; the com-
panion-hatch, which led to the deck below, was
betwixt the after-end of the cabin and the bulkhead
of the berth, but the rapid glance I threw around
speedily settled, as you may suppose, into a look—a
long look—full of curiosity, surprise, and admiration,
at the girl.

She stood before me dressed as a sailor lad, in a suit
of pilot cloth and a red silk handkerchief round her

throat ; but her first act on entering was to remove
her cloth cap, that was streaming wet, and throw it
down upon the table ; and thus she stood with her
eyes fixed on me, as mine were on her, each of us surveying the other. Her hair was cut short, and was
rough and plentiful, without remains of any sort of
fashion in the wearing of it—nay, indeed, it was un-
parted. It was very fair hair, and as pale as amber in
the lamplight. Her eyebrows were of a darker colour,
and very perfectly arched, as though pencilled. It was
impossible to guess the hue of her eyes by that light :
they seemed of a very dark blue, such as might prove
violet in the sunshine, soft and liquid, and of an expression, even in that hour of peril, of the horror of
tempest, of the prospect of death, indeed, that might
make one readily suppose her of a nature both sweet
and merry. There was no sign of exposure to the
weather upon her face ; she was white with the pale-
ness of fatigue and emotion. Her cheeks were plump,
her mouth small, the under-lip a little pouted, and her
teeth pearl-like and very regular. Even by the light
in which I now surveyed her, I never for a moment
could have mistaken her for a lad. There was

nothing in her garb to neutralize for an instant the suggestions of her sex.

' I will take you to my father,' said she ; ' but you must first eat and drink.'

I could not have told how exhausted I was until I sank down upon a locker and rested my arms upon the table. I was too wearied to ask the questions that I should have put to her at another time, and could do no more than watch her, with a sort of dull wonder at her nimbleness, and the spirit and resolution of her movements as she lifted the lid of the locker and produced a case-bottle of Hollands, some cold meat, and a tin of white biscuits.

' We have no bread,' said she, smiling ; ' we obtained some loaves off the Isle of Wight, but the last was eaten yesterday.'

She took a tumbler from a rack and mixed a draught of the Hollands with some water which she got from a filter fixed to a stanchion, and extended the glass.

' Pray let me follow you !' said I. She shook her head. ' Yes !' I cried ; ' God knows you should need some such tonic more than I !'

I induced her to drink, and then took the glass and emptied it. A second dram warmed and heartened me. I was without appetite, but was willing to eat for the sake of such strength as might come from a meal. The girl made herself a sandwich of biscuit and meat, and we fell to. And so we sat facing each other, eating, staring at each other ; the pair of us all the while hearkening with all our ears to the roaring noises outside, to the straining sounds within the ship, and feeling—I speak of myself·—with every nerve tense as a fiddlestring, the desperate slants and falls and uprisals of the deck or platform upon which our feet rested.

CHAPTER V.

THERE was refreshment, however, to every sense, beyond language to express, in the shelter which this deck-house provided after our long term of exposure to the pouring of the raging gale, into which was put the further weight of volumes of spray, that swept to the face like leaden hail, and carried the shriek of the shot of musketry as it slung past the ear. It was calm in this deck-house; the deafening sounds without came somewhat muffled here; but the furious motion of the vessel was startlingly illustrated by the play of the hanging lantern, and the swing of the illuminated globe was made the wilder and more wonderful by the calm of the atmosphere in which it oscillated.

'I do not think the sea is breaking over the ship,'

said the girl, gazing at me in a posture of listening.
' It is hard to tell.   I feel no tremble as of the falls
of water on the deck.'

' She is battling bravely,' said I ; ' but what now
would I give for even a couple of those men of yours
who jumped into the lifeboat ! It is our being so few—
two of us only, and you a woman—that makes our
situation so hard.'

' I have not the strength of a man,' said she with a
smile, and fastening her soft eyes on my face ; ' but you
will find I have the heart of one.   Will you come
now and see my father ?'

I at once rose and followed her.   She knocked
upon a little door where the bulkhead partitioned
off the inner cabin, and then entered, bidding me
follow her.

A cot swung from the upper deck, and in it sat
a man almost upright, his back supported by bolsters
and pillows ; a bracket lamp burnt steadily over a
table, upon which lay a book or two, a chart, a few
nautical instruments, and the like.   There was no
convenience for dressing, and I guessed that this had
been a sort of chart-room which the captain had

chosen to occupy that he might be easily and without delay within hail or reach of the deck.

He was a striking-looking man, with coal-black hair, parted on one side, lying very flat upon his head, and curling down upon his back. He wore a long goat beard and moustaches, and was somewhat grim with several days' growth of whisker upon his cheeks ; his brows were thickly thatched, his forehead low, his eyes very dark, small, and penetrating. He was of a death-like whiteness, and showed, to my fancy, as a man whose days were numbered. That his disease was something more than rheumatism there was no need to look at him twice to make sure of. His daughter addressed him in the Danish tongue, then, recollecting herself, with a half-glance at me of apology, she exclaimed :

'Father, this is Mr. Hugh Tregarthen, the noble gentleman who commanded the lifeboat, who risked his life to save ours, and I pray that God of His love for brave spirits may restore him in safety to those who are dear to him.'

Captain Nielsen, with a face contracted into a look of pain by emotion, extended his hand in silence over the edge of his cot. I grasped it in silence too. It was ice cold. He gazed for awhile, without speech, into my eyes, and I thought to see him shed tears ; then, putting his hand upon mine in a caressing gesture, and letting it go—for the swing of the cot would not permit him to retain that posture of hold- ing my hand for above a moment or two, he ex- claimed in a low but quite audible voice : 'I ask the good and gracious Lord of heaven and earth to bless you, for *her* sake—for my Helga's sake—and in the name of those who have perished, but whom you would have saved !'

'Captain Nielsen,' said I, greatly moved by his manner and looks, 'would it had pleased Heaven that I should have been of solid use to you and your men ! I grieve to find you in this helpless state. I hope you do not suffer ?'

'While I rest I am without pain,' he answered, and I now observed that though his accent had a distinctly Scandinavian harshness, such as was softened in his daughter's speech by the clearness—I may say, by the melody—of her tones, his English was as purely pronounced as hers. 'But if I move,' he continued,

'I am in agony. I cannot stand; my legs are as idle and as helpless as though paralyzed. But now tell me of the *Anine*, Helga,' he cried, with a look of pathetic eager yearning entering his face as he addressed her. 'Have you sounded the well?'

'Yes, father.'

'What water, my child?' She told him. 'Ha!' he exclaimed, with a sudden fretfulness; 'the pump should be manned without delay; but who is there to work it?'

'We two will, very shortly,' she exclaimed, turning to me: 'we require a little breathing time. Mr. Tregarthen and I,' said she, still talking with her soft appealing eyes upon me, 'have strength, or, at all events, courage enough to give us strength; and he will help me in whatever we may think needful to save the *Anine* and our lives.'

'Indeed, yes!' said I.

'Pray sit, both of you,' cried Captain Nielsen; 'pray rest. Helga, have you seen to the gentleman's comfort? Has he had any refreshment?'

She answered him, and seated herself upon a little locker, inviting me with a look to sit beside her, for there was no other accommodation in that cabin than the locker.

'I wish I could persuade your daughter to take some rest,' said I. 'Her clothes, too, are soaked through !'

'It is salt water,' said Captain Nielsen; 'it will not harm her. She is very used to salt water, sir;' and then he addressed his daughter in Danish. The resemblance of some words he used to our English made me suppose he spoke about her resting.

'The pumps must be worked,' said she, looking at me; 'we must keep the barque afloat first of all, Mr. Tregarthen. How trifling is want of sleep, how insignificant the discomfort of damp clothes, at such a time as this !'

She opened her jacket and drew a silver watch from her pocket, and then took a bottle of medicine and a wineglass from a small circular tray swinging by thin chains near the cot, and gave her father a dose. He began now to question us, occasionally in his hurry and eagerness speaking in the Danish language. He asked about the masts—if they were sound, if any sails had been split, if the *Anine* had met with any injury apart from the loss of her two boats, of which he had evidently been informed by his daughter. A flush of temper came into his white cheeks when he talked of his men. He called the carpenter Damm a villain, said that had he had his way the barque never would have brought up in that bay, that Damm had carried her there, as he now believed, as much out of spite as out of recklessness, hoping no doubt that the *Anine* would go ashore, but of course taking it for granted that the crew would be rescued. He shook his fist as he pronounced the carpenter's name, and then groaned aloud with anguish to some movement of his limbs brought about by his agitation. He lay quiet a little and grew calm, and talked, with his thin fingers on his breast. He informed me that the *Anine* was his ship, that he had spent some hundreds of pounds in equipping her for this voyage, that he had some risk in the cargo, and that, in a word, all that he was worth in the wide world was in this fabric, now heavily and often madly labouring, unwatched, amid the blackness of the night of hurricane. ·

'Your daughter and I must endeavour to preserve her for you,' said I.

'May the blessed God grant it!' he cried. 'And how good and heroic are you to speak thus!' said he, looking at me. 'Surely your great Nelson was right when he called us Danes the brothers of the English. Brothers in affection may our countries ever be! We have given you a sweet Princess—that is a debt it will tax your people's generosity to repay.' The smile that lighted up his face as he spoke made me see a resemblance in him to his daughter. It was like throwing a light upon a picture. He was now looking at her with an expression full of tenderness and concern.

'Mr.—Mr.——' he began.

'Tregarthen,' said his daughter.

'Ay, Mr. Tregarthen,' he continued, ' will wonder that a girl should be clad as you are, Helga. Were you ever in Denmark, sir?'

'Never,' I replied.

'You will not suppose, I hope,' said he, with another soft, engaging smile that was pathetic also with the meaning it took from his white face, 'that Helga's attire is the costume of Danish ladies?'

'Oh no,' said I. 'I see how it is. Indeed, Miss Nielsen explained. The dress is a whim. And then it is a very convenient shipboard dress. But she should not be suffered to do the rough work of a sailor. Will you believe, Captain Nielsen, that she went out upon the bowsprit, and cut adrift or loosed the staysail there when your barque was on her beam-ends in the trough of the sea?'

He nodded with emphasis, and said, 'That is nothing. Helga has been to sea with me now for six years running. It is her delight to dress herself in boy's clothes—ay, and to go aloft and do the work of a seaman. It has hardened and spoilt her hands, but it has left her face fair to see. She is a good girl; she loves her poor father; she is motherless, Mr. Tregarthen. Were my dear wife alive, Helga would not be here. She is my only child;' and he made as if to extend his arms to her, but immediately crossed his hands, again addressing her in Danish as though he blessed her.

I could perceive the spirit in her struggling with the weakness that this talk induced. She conquered her emotions with a glance at me that was one almost of pride, as though she would bid me observe that she was mistress of herself, and said, changing the

8—2

subject, but not abruptly, ' Father, do you think the vessel can struggle on without being watched or helped from the deck ?'

' What can be done?' he cried. ' The helm is securely lashed hard a-lee ?' She nodded. ' What can be done ?' he repeated. ' Your standing at the wheel would be of no use. What is the trim of the yards ?'

' They lie as they were braced up in the bay,' she responded.

' I have been in ships,' said he, ' that always managed best when left alone in hard weather of this kind. There was the old *Dannebrog,*' he went on, with his eyes seeming to glisten to some sudden stir of happy memory in him. ' Twice when I was in her—once in the Baltic, once in the South Atlantic —we met with gales : well, perhaps not such a gale as this ; but it blew very fiercely, Mr. Tregarthen. The captain, my old friend Sorensen, knew her as he knew his wife. He pointed the yards, lashed the helm, sent the crew below and waited, smoking his pipe in the cabin, till the weather broke. She climbed the seas dryly, and no whale could have made better weather of it. A ship has an intelligence of her own. It is the spirit of the sea that comes into her, as into the birds or fish of the ocean. Observe how long a vessel will wash about after her crew have abandoned her. They might have sunk her had they stayed, not understanding her. Much must be left to chance at sea, Helga. No; there is nothing to be done. Damm reported the hatch-covers on and everything secure while in the bay. It is so still, of course. Yet it will ease my mind to know she is a little freed of the water in her.'

'I am ready!' cried I. 'Is the pump too heavy for my arms alone? I cannot bear to think of your daughter toiling upon that wet and howling deck.'

'She will not spare herself, though you should wish it,' said her father. 'What is the hour, my dear?'

She looked at her watch. 'Twenty minutes after two.'

'A weary long time yet to wait for the dawn!' said he. 'And it is Sunday morning—a day of rest for all the world save for the mariner. But it is God's own day, and when next Sabbath comes round we may be worshipping Him ashore, and thanking Him for our preservation.'

As he pronounced these words, Helga, as I will henceforth call her, giving me a glance of invitation, quitted the berth, and I followed her into the cabin, as I may term the interior of the deck-house. She picked up the bull's-eye lamp and trimmed the mesh of it, and, arming herself with the sounding-rod, stepped on to the deck. I watched her movements with astonishment and admiration. I should have believed that I possessed fairly good sea-legs, even for a wilder play of plank than this which was now tossing us ; nevertheless, I never dared let go with my hands, and there were moments when the upheaval was so swift, the fall so sickening, that my brain reeled again, and to have saved my life I could not have stirred the distance of a pace until the sensation had passed. But excepting an occa-sional pause, an infrequent grasp at what was next her during some unusually heavy roll, Helga moved with almost the same sort of ease that must have been visible in her on a level floor. Her figure, indeed, seemed to float ; it swayed to the rolling of the deck as a flame hovers upright upon the candle you sharply sway under it.

After the comparative calm of the shelter I stepped from, the uproar of the gale sounded as though it were blowing as hard again as at the time of our quitting the deck. The noise of the rushing and roaring waters was deafening; as the vessel brought her masts to windward, the screaming and whistling aloft are not to be imagined. The wind was clouded with spray, the decks sobbed furiously with wet, and it was still as pitch black as ever it had been at any hour of the night. Helga threw the light of the bull's-eye upon the pump-brake or handle, and we then fell to work. At intervals we could contrive to hear each other speak—that is to say, in some momentary lull, when the barque was in the heart of a valley ere she rose to the next thunderous acclivity, yelling in her rigging with the voice of a wounded giantess. For how long we stuck to that dismal clanking job I cannot remember. The water gushed copiously as we plied the handle, and the foam was all about our feet as though we stood in a half-fathom's depth of surf. I was amazed by the endurance and pluck of the girl, and, indeed, I found half my strength in her courage. Had I been alone I am persuaded I should have given up. The blow of the wheel that had dashed me into unconsciousness, coming on top of my previous labours, not to speak of that exhaustion of mind which follows upon such distress of heart as my situation and the memory of my foundered boat and the possible loss of all her people had occasioned in me, must have proved too much but for the example and influence, the inspiriting presence of this little Danish lioness, Helga.

In one of those intervals I have spoken of she cried out, ' We have done enough—for the present ;' and so saying she let go of the pump-handle and asked me to hold the lamp while she dropped the rod. I had supposed our efforts insignificant, and was surprised to learn that we had sunk the water by some inches. We returned to the deck-house, but scarcely had I entered it when I was seized with exhaustion so prostrating that I fell, rather than seated myself, upon the locker and hid my face in my arms upon the table till the sudden darkness should have passed from my eyes. When, presently, I looked up, I found Helga at my side with a glass of spirits in her hand. There was a wonderful anxiety and compassion in her gaze.

'Drink this!' said she. 'The work has been too hard for you. It is my fault—I am sorry—I am sorry.'

I swallowed the draught, and was the better for it.

'This weakness,' said I, 'must come from the blow I got on deck. I have kept you from your father. He will want your report,' and I stood up.

She gave me her arm, and but for that support I believe I should not have been able to make my way to the captain's berth, so weak did I feel in the limbs, so paralyzing to my condition of prostration was the violent motion of the deck.

Captain Nielsen looked eagerly at us over the edge of his cot. Helga would not release me until I was seated on the locker.

'Mr. Tregarthen's strength has been overtaxed, father,' said she.

'Poor man! poor man!' he cried. 'God will bless him. He has suffered much for us.'

'It must be a weakness, following my having been

stunned,' said I, ashamed of myself that I should
be in need of a girl's pity at such a time—the
pity of a girl, too, who was sharing my labours and
danger.

' What have you to tell me, Helga?' exclaimed the
captain.

She answered him in Danish, and they exchanged
some sentences in that tongue.

' She is a tight ship,' cried the captain, addressing
me : ' it is good news,' he went on, his white countenance lighted up with an expression of exultation.
' to hear that you two should be able to control
the water in the hold. Does the weather seem to
moderate ?'

' No,' said I ; ' it blows as hard as ever it did.'

' Does the sea break aboard ?'

' There is plenty of water washing about,' said
I, ' but the vessel seems to be making a brave
fight.'

' When daylight comes, Helga,' said he, ' you will
hoist a distress colour at the mizzen-peak. If the
peak be wrecked or the halliards gone, the flag must
be seized to the mizzen shrouds.'

'I will see to all that, father,' she answered; 'and now, Mr. Tregarthen, you will take some rest.'

I could not bear the idea of sleeping while she remained up; yet though neither of us could be of the least use on deck, our both resting at once was not to be thought of, if it was only for the sake of the comfort that was to be got out of knowing that there was somebody awake and on watch.

'I will gladly rest,' said I, 'on condition that you now lie down and sleep for two or three hours.'

She answered no; she was less tired than I; she had not undergone what I had suffered in the lifeboat. She begged me to take some repose.

'It is my selfishness that entreats you,' said she: 'if you break down, what are my father and I to do?'

'True,' I exclaimed, 'but the three of us would be worse off still if *you* were to break down.'

However, as I saw that she was very much in earnest, while her father also joined her in entreating me to rest, I consented on her agreeing first to remove her soaking clothes, for it was miserable to see her shivering from time to time and looking as though she had just been dragged over the side, and yet bravely disregarding the discomfort, smiling as often as she addressed me and conversing with her father with a face of serenity, plainly striving to soothe and reassure him by an air of cheerful confidence.

She left the cabin, and Captain Nielsen talked of her at once : told me that her mother was an Englishwoman ; that he was married in London, in which city he had lived from time to time ; that Helga had received a part of her education at Newcastle-on-Tyne, where his wife's family then lived, though they were now scattered, or perhaps dead, only one member to his knowledge still residing at Newcastle. He took Helga to sea with him, he said, after his wife died, that he might have her under his eye, and such was her love for the sea, such her intelligent interest in everything which concerned a ship, that she could do as much with a vessel as he himself, and had often, at her own request, taken charge for a watch, during which she had shortened canvas and put the craft about as though, in short, she had been skipper. The poor

man seemed to forget his miserable situation while
he spoke of Helga. His heart was full of her; his
eyes swam with tears while he cried, 'It is not
that I fear death for myself, nor for myself do I
dread the loss of my ship, which would signify
beggary for me and my child. It is for her—for
my little Helga. We have friends at Kolding, where
I was born, and at Bjert, Vonsild, Skandrup, and
at other places. But who will help the orphan?
My friends are not rich—they could do little, no
matter how generous their will. I pray God, for
my child's sake, that we may be preserved—ay, and
for your sake—I should have said that,' he added,
feebly smiling, though his face was one of distress.

He was beginning to question me about my home,
and I was telling him that my mother was living,
and that she and I were alone in the world, and
that I feared she would think me drowned, and
grieve till her heart broke, for she was an old
lady, and I was her only son, as Helga was his only
daughter, when the girl entered, and I broke off.
She had changed her attire, but her clothes were
still those of a lad. I had thought to see her come

in dressed as a woman, and she so interpreted the look I fastened upon her, for she at once said, without the least air of confusion, as though, indeed, she were sensible of nothing in her apparel that demanded an excuse from her: 'I must preserve my sailor's garb until the fine weather comes. How should I be able to move about the decks in a gown ?'

'Helga,' cried her father, 'Mr. Tregarthen is the only son of his mother, and she awaits his return.'

Instantly entered an expression of beautiful compassion into her soft eyes. Her gaze fell, and she remained for a few moments silent; the lamplight shone upon her tumbled hair, and I am without words to make you see the sweet sorrowful expression of her pale face as she stood close against the door, silent, and looking down.

'I have kept my word, Mr. Tregarthen,' said she presently. 'Now you will keep yours and rest yourself. There is my father's cabin below.'

I interrupted her: 'No; if you please, I will lie down upon one of the lockers in the deck-house.'

'It will make a hard bed,' said she.

'Not too hard for me,' said I.

'Well, you shall lie down upon one of those lockers, and you shall be comfortable too;' and, saying this, she went out again, and shortly afterwards returned with some rugs and a bolster. These she placed upon the lee locker, and a minute or two later I had shaken the poor captain by the hand, and had stretched myself upon the rugs, where I lay listening to the thunder of the gale and following the wild motions of the barque, and thinking of what had happened since the lifeboat summons had rung me into this black, and frothing, and roaring night from my snug fireside.

It was not long, however, before I fell asleep. I had undergone some lifeboat experiences in my time, but never before was nature so exhausted in me. The roaring of the gale, the cannonading of the deck-house by incessant heavy showerings of water, the extravagant motions of the plunging and rolling vessel, might have been a mother's lullaby sung by the side of a gently-rocked cradle, so deep was the slumber these sounds of thunder left unvexed.

I awoke from a dreamless, deathlike sleep, and

opened my eyes against the light of the cold stone-
gray dawn, and my mind instantly coming to me,
I sprang up from the locker, pausing to guess at
the weather from the movement and the sound.
It was still blowing a whole gale of wind, and I
was unable to stand without grasping the table for
support. The deck-house door was shut, and the
planks within were dry, though I could hear the
water gushing and pouring in the alleys betwixt
the deck-house and the bulwarks. I thought
to take a view of the weather through one of the
windows, but the glass was everywhere blind with
wet.

At this moment the door of the captain's berth was
opened, and Helga stepped out. She immediately
approached me with both hands extended in the
most cordial manner imaginable.

'You have slept well,' she cried ; ' I bent over you
three or four times. You are the better for the rest,
I am sure.'

' I am, indeed !' said I. ' And you ?'

' Oh, I shall sleep by-and-by. What shall we
do for hot water ? It is impossible to light the galley

fire ; yet how grateful would be a cup of hot tea or coffee !'

' Have you been on deck,' said I, ' while I slept ?'

' Oh yes, in and out,' she answered. ' All is well so far—I mean, the *Anine* goes on making a brave fight. The dawn has not long broken. I have not yet seen the ship by daylight. We must sound the well, Mr. Tregarthen, before we break our fast— my fear is there,' she added, pointing to the deck, by which she signified the hold.

There was but little of her face to be seen. She was wearing an indiarubber cap shaped like a sou'-wester, the brim of which came low, while the flannel ear-flaps almost smothered her cheeks. I could now see, however, that her eyes were of a dark blue, with a spirit of life and even of vivacity in them that expressed a wonderful triumph of heart over the languor of frame indicated by the droop of the eye-lids. A little of her short hair of pale gold showed under the hinder thatch of the sou'-wester ; her face was blanched. But I could not look at the pretty mouth, the pearl-like teeth, the soft blue eyes, the delicately figured nostril, without guessing that in the hour of bloom this girl would show as bonnily as the fairest lass of cream and roses that ever hailed from Denmark.

We stepped on to the deck—into the thunder of the gale and the flying clouds of spray. I still wore my oilskins, and was as dry in them as at the hour of leaving home. I felt the comfort, I assure you, of my high sea-boots as I stood upon that deck, holding on a minute to the house-front, with the water coming in a little rage of froth to my legs and washing to leeward with the *scend* of the barque with the force of a river overflowing a dam.

Our first glance was aloft. The foretopgallant-mast was broken off at the head of the topmast and hung with its two yards supported by its gear, but giving a strange wrecked look to the whole of the fabric up there as it swung to the headlong movements of the hull, making the spars, down to the solid foot of the foremast, tremble with the spearing blows it dealt. The jibbooms were also gone, and this, no doubt, had happened through the carrying away of the topgallant-mast ; otherwise all was right up above, assuming, to be sure, that

nothing was sprung. But the wild, soaked, desolate—
the almost mutilated—look, indeed, of the barque!
How am I to communicate the impression produced
by the soaked dark lines of sailcloth rolled upon
the yards, the ends of rope blowing out like the
pennant of a man-of-war, the arched and gleaming
gear, the decks dusky with incessant drenchings
and emitting sullen flashes as the dark flood upon
them rolled from side to side! The running rigging
lay all about, working like serpents in the wash of the
water ; from time to time a sea would strike the bow
and burst on high in steam-like volumes which
glanced ghastly against the leaden sky that overhung us in strata of scowling vapour, dark as thunder
in places, yet seemingly motionless. A furious
Atlantic sea was running ; it came along in hills
of frothing green which shaped themselves out of
a near horizon thick with storms of spume. But
there was the regularity of the unfathomed ocean
in the run of the surge, mountainous as it was ; and
the barque, with her lashed helm, not a rag showing
save a tatter or two of the fore-topmast-staysail whose
head we had exposed on the previous night, soared

and sank, with her port bow to the sea, with the regularity of the tick of a clock.

There was nothing in sight. I looked eagerly round the sea, but it was all thickness and foam and headlong motion. We went aft to the compass to observe if there had happened any shift in the wind, and what the trend of the barque was, and also to note the condition of the wheel, which could only have been told in the darkness by groping. The helm was perfectly sound, and the lashings held bravely. I could observe now that the wheel was a small one, formed of brass, also that it worked the rudder by means of a screw, and it was this purchase or leverage, I suppose, that had made me find the barque easy to steer while she was scudding. The gale was blowing fair out of the north-east, and the vessel's trend, therefore, was on a dead south-west course, with the help of a mountainous sea besides, to drive her away from the land, beam on. I cried to Helga that I thought our drift would certainly not be less than four, and perhaps five, miles in the hour. She watched the sea for a little, and then nodded to me; but it was scarcely likely that she could conjecture the rate of progress amid so furious a commotion of waters, with the great seas boiling to the bulwark rail, and rushing away to leeward in huge round backs of freckled green.

She was evidently too weary to talk, rendered too languid by the bitter cares and sleepless hours of the long night to exert her voice so as to be audible in that thunder of wind which came flashing over the side in guns and bursts of hurricane power; and to the few sentences I uttered, or rather shouted, she responded by nods and shakes of the head as it might be. There was a flag locker under the gratings abaft the wheel, and she opened the box, took out a small Danish ensign, bent it on to the peak-signal halliards, and between us we ran it half-mast high, and there it stood, hard and firm as a painted board, a white cross on red ground, and the red of it made it resemble a tongue of fire against the soot of the sky. This done, we returned to the main-deck, and Helga sounded the pump. She went to work with all the expertness of a seasoned salt, carefully dried the rod and chalked it, and then waited until the roll of the barque brought

her to a level keel before dropping it. I watched her
with astonishment and admiration. It would until
now have seemed impossible to me that any mortal
woman should have had in her the makings of so
nimble and practised a sailor as I found her to be,
with nothing, either, of the tenderness of girlhood lost
in her, in speech, in countenance, in looks, spite
of her boy's clothes. She examined the rod, and
eyed me with a grave countenance.

' Does the water gain ?' said I.

' There are two more inches of it,' she answered,
' than the depth I found in the hold last night when
I first sounded. We ought to free her somewhat.'

' I am willing,' I exclaimed ; 'but are you equal
to such labour ? A couple of hours should not make
a very grave difference.'

' No, no !' she interrupted, with a vehemence that
put her air of weariness to flight. ' A couple of hours
would be too long to wait,' saying which she grasped
the brake and we went to work as before.

No one who has not had to labour in this way can
conceive the fatigue of it. There is no sort of ship-
board work that more quickly exhausts. It grieved

me to the soul that my associate in this toil should
be a girl, with the natural weakness of her sex
accentuated by what she had suffered and was
still suffering ; but her spirited gaze forbade remon-
strance. She seemed scarcely able to stand when
utter weariness forced her at last to let go of the
brake. Nevertheless, she compelled her feeble hands
again to drop the rod down the well. We had
reduced the water to the height at which we had left
it before, and, with a faint smile of congratulation, she
made a movement towards the deck-house ; but her
gait was so staggering, there was such a character of
blindness, too, in her posture as she started to walk,
that I grasped her arm and, indeed, half carried her
into the house.

She sat and rested herself for a few minutes, but
appeared unable to speak. I watched her anxiously,
with something of indignation that her father, who
professed to love her so dearly, should not come
between her and her devotion, and insist upon her
resting. Presently she rose and walked to his cabin,
telling me with her looks to follow her.

CHAPTER VI.

CAPTAIN NIELSEN was veritably corpse-like in aspect viewed by the cold gray iron light sifting through the little windows out of the spray-shrouded air. The unnatural brightness of his eyes painfully defined the attenuation of his face, and the sickly, parchment-like complexion of his skin. He extended his hand, but could hardly find time to deliver a greeting, so violent was his hurry to receive his daughter's report. He shook his head when he heard that his top-gallant-mast and jibbooms were wrecked, and passion-ately exclaimed in Danish, on his daughter telling him of the increase of water in the hold.

·'She must be taking it in from below,' he then cried in English. 'She has strained herself. Should this continue, what is to be done? She will need to be constantly pumped—and ah, my God! you are but two.'

'Yes, Captain,' cried I, incensed that he should appear to have no thoughts but for his ship; 'but if you do not insist upon your daughter taking some rest there will be but one, long before this gale has blown itself out.'

'Oh, my dear, it is so!' he exclaimed, looking at her on a sudden with impassioned concern. 'Mr. Tregarthen is right. You will sink under your efforts. Your dear heart will break. Rest now— rest, my beloved child! I command you to rest! You must go below: you must lie in your own cabin. This good gentleman is about—he will sit with me and go forth and report. The *Anine* tends herself, and there is nothing in human skill to help her out-side what she can herself do.'

'But we must not starve, father,' she answered: 'let us first breakfast, as best we can, and then I will go below.'

She left the cabin and promptly returned, bringing with her the remains of the cold meat we had supped off, some biscuit, and a bottle of red wine. Her father drank a little of the wine and ate a morsel of biscuit; indeed, food seemed to excite a loathing in him. I saw that Helga eyed him piteously, but she did not press him to eat: it might be that she had experience of his stubbornness. She said, in a soft aside, to me: 'His appetite is leaving him, and how can I tempt him without the means of cooking? Does not he look very ill this morning?'

'It is worry, added to rheumatic pains,' said I: 'we must get him ashore as soon as possible, where he can be nursed in comfort.'

But though these words flowed readily, out of my sympathy with the poor, brave, suffering girl, they were assuredly not in correspondence with my secret feelings. It was not only I was certain that Captain Nielsen lay in his cot a dying man; the roaring of the wind, the beating of the sea against the barque, the wild extravagant leapings and divings, the perception that water was draining into the hold, and that there were but two of us—and one of those two a girl—to work the pumps, made a mockery to my heart of my reference to the Captain getting ashore and being nursed there.

We sat in that slanting and leaping interior with plates on our knees. The girl feigned to eat; her head drooped with weariness, yet I noticed that she would force a cheerful note into the replies she made to her father's ceaseless feverish questions. When we had ended our meal, she left us to go below to her cabin; but before leaving she asked me, with eyes full of tender pleading, to keep her father's heart up, to make the best of such reports as I might have to give him after going out to take a look round; and she told me that he would need his physic at such and such a time, and so lingered, dwelling upon him and glancing at him; and then she went out in a hurry with one hand upon her breast, yet not so swiftly but that I could see her eyes were swimming.

'There is a barometer in the cabin,' said Captain Nielsen; 'will you tell me how the mercury stands?'

The glass was fixed to the bulkhead outside. I returned and gave him the reading.

''Tis a little rise!' he cried, with his unnaturally bright eyes eagerly fastened upon me.

I would not tell him that it was not so—that the mercury, indeed, stood at the level I had observed on the preceding day in my glass in the lifeboat house.

'Fierce weather of this sort,' said I, 'soon exhausts itself.'

He continued to stare at me, but now with an air of musing that somewhat softened the painful brilliant intentness of his regard.

'I pray God,' said he, 'that this weather may speedily enable us to obtain help, for I fear that if I am not treated I shall get very low, perhaps die. I am ill—yet what is my malady? This rheumatism is a sudden seizure. I could walk when at Cuxhaven.'

In as cheerful a voice as I could assume, I begged him to consider that his mind might have much to do with those bodily sensations which made him feel ill.

'It may be so, it may be so,' he exclaimed, with a sad smile of faltering hope. 'I wish to live. I am not an old man. It will be hard if my time is to come soon. It is Helga—it is Helga,' he muttered, pressing his brow with his thin hand. I was about to speak. 'How wearisome,' he broke out, 'is this ceaseless tossing! I ran away to sea; it was my own doing. I had my childish dreams — strange and beautiful fancies of foreign countries—and I ran away;' he went on in a rambling manner like one thinking aloud. 'And yet I love the old ocean, though it is serving me cruelly now. It has fed me— it has held me to its breast—and my nourishment and life have come from it.' He started, and, bringing his eyes away from the upper deck on which they had been fixed while he spoke, he cried, 'Sir, you are a stranger to me, but you are an Englishman of heroic heart, and you will forgive me. Should I die, and should God be pleased to spare you and my child, will you protect her until she has safely returned to her friends at Kolding? She will be alone in any part of the world until she is there, and if I am assured that she will have the generous compassion of your heart with her, a guardian to take my place until she reaches Kolding, it will make me easy in my ending, let the stroke come when it will.'

'I came to this ship to save your lives,' I answered. 'I hope to be an instrument yet of helping to save them. Trust me to do your bidding, if it were only for my admiration of your daughter's heroic qualities. But do not speak of dying, Captain Nielsen——'

He interrupted me. 'There is my dear friend Pastor Blicker of Kolding, and there is Pastor Jansen of Skandrup. They are good and gentle Christian men, who will receive Helga, and stand by her and soothe her and counsel her as to my little property—ah, my little property!' he cried. 'If this vessel founders, what have I?'

'Pray,' said I, with the idea of quietly coaxing his mind into a more cheerful mood, 'what is so seriously wrong with you, Captain, that you should lie there gloomily foreboding your death? Such rheumatism as yours is not very quick to kill.'

'I was long dangerously ill of a fever in the West Indies,' he answered, 'and it left a vital organ weak. The mischief is here, I fear,' said he, touching his right side above his hip. 'I felt very ill at Cuxhaven; but this voyage was to be made; I am too poor a man to suffer my health to forfeit the money that is to be got by it. Hark! what was that?'

He leaned his head over the cot, straining his hearing with a nervous fluttering of his emaciated fingers. It was miserable to see how white the skin of his sunken cheeks showed against the whiteness of the canvas of his cot.

'I heard nothing,' I answered.

'It was the noise of a blow,' he exclaimed. 'Pray go and see if anything is wrong,' he added, speaking out of his habit of giving orders, and with a peremptoriness that forced a smile from me as I went to the door.

I made my way through the house on to the deck, and looked about me, but it was the same scene to stare at and hearken to that I had viewed before: the same thunder and shriek of wind, the same clouding of the forward part of the barque in foam, the same miserable dismal picture of water flashing from bulwark to bulwark, of high green frothing seas towering past the line of the rail as the vessel swung in a smother of seething yeast into the trough.

I caught sight of a long hencoop abaft the structure in which the sailors had lived, with the red gleam of a cockscomb betwixt a couple of the bars, and guessing that the wretched inmates must, by this time, be in sore need of food and water, I very cautiously made my way to the coop, holding on by something at

every step. The coop was, indeed, full of poultry, but
all lay drowned.

I returned to the deck-house and mounted on top
of it, where I should be able to obtain a good view of
as much of the ocean as was exposed, and where also
I should be out of the wet which, on the main deck,
rolled with weight enough at times to sweep a man
off his legs. The roof of the house, if I may so term
it, was above the rail, and the whole fury of the gale
swept across it. I never could have guessed at the
hurricane-force of the wind while standing on the
deck beneath. It was impossible to face it; if I
glanced but one instant to windward my eyes seemed
to be blown into my head.

I had not gained that elevation above a minute
when I heard a sharp rattling aloft, and, looking upwards, I perceived that the main royal had blown
loose. For the space of a breath or two it made the
rattling noise that had called my attention to it, then
the whole bladder-like body of it was swept in a flash
away from the yard, and nothing remained but a
whip or two streaming straight out like white hair
from the spar. A moment later the maintopgallant-

sail, that had been, no doubt, hastily and badly furled, was blown out of the gaskets. I thought to see it go as the royal had, but while I watched, waiting for the flight of the rags of it down into the leeward gloom of the sky, the mast snapped off at the cap at the instant of the sail bursting and disappearing like a gush of mist, and down fell the whole mass of hamper to a little below the stay, under which it madly swung, held by its gear.

This disaster, comparatively trifling as it was, gave the whole fabric a most melancholy, wrecked look. It affected me in a manner I should not have thought possible in one who knew so much about the sea and shipwreck as I. It impressed me as an omen of approaching dissolution. 'What, in God's name, can save us?' I remember thinking, as I brought my eyes away from the two broken masts, swinging and spearing high up under the smoke-coloured, compacted, apparently stirless heaps of vapour stretching from sea-line to sea-line. 'What put together by mortal hands can go on resisting this ceaseless, tremendous beating?' and as I thus thought the vessel, with a wild sweep of her bow, smote a giant surge rushing laterally at her, and a whole green sea broke roaring over the forecastle, making every timber in her tremble with a volcanic thrill, and entirely submerging the forepart in white waters, out of which she soared with a score of cataracts flying in smoke from her sides.

I looked for the flag that Helga and I had halfmasted a little while before; it had as utterly disappeared from betwixt its toggles as though the bunting had been ripped up and down by a knife. As I was in the act of dragging myself along to the ladder to go below, I spied a sort of smudge oozing out of the iron-hued thickness past the head of a great sea whose arching peak was like a snow-clad hill. I crouched down to steady myself, and presently what I had at first thought to be some dark shadow of cloud upon the near horizon grew into the proportions of a large ship, running dead before the gale under a narrow band of main-topsail.

She was heading to pass under our stern, and rapidly drew out, and in a few minutes I had her clear—clean and bright as a new painting against the background of shadow, along whose dingy, misty base

the ocean line was washing in flickering green heights.
She was a large steam frigate, clearly a foreigner, for
I do not know that our country had a ship of the
kind afloat at the time. She had a white band
broken by ports, and the black and gleaming defences
of her bulwarks were crowned with stowed hammocks.
Her topgallant-masts were housed, and the large
cross-trees and huge black tops and wide spread of
shrouds gave her a wonderfully heavy, massive ship-
of-war look aloft. The band of close-reefed main-
topsail had the glare of foam as it swung majestically
from one sea-line to the other, slowly swaying across
the dark and stooping heaven with a noble and
solemn rhythm of movement. I never could have
imagined a sight to more wholly fascinate my gaze.
Always crouching low, I watched her under the
shelter of my hands locked upon my brow. I beheld
nothing living aboard of her. She came along as
though informed by some spirit and government of
her own. As her great stem sank to the figure-head,
there arose a magnificent boiling, a mountainous
cloud of froth on either bow of her, and the roar of
those riven seas seemed to add a deeper tone of

thunder to the gale. All was taut aboard—every
rope like a ruled line—different, indeed, from our
torn and wrecked and trailing appearance on high!
She swept past within a quarter of a mile of us, and
what pen could convey the incredible power suggested
by that great fabric as her stern lifted to the curl of
the enormous Atlantic surge, and the whole ship
rushed forward on the hurling froth of the sea with
an electric velocity that brought the very heart into
one's throat.

She was a mere smudge again—this time to leeward—in a few minutes. I could only stare at her.
Our flag had blown away, I was without power to
signal, and, even if I had been able to communicate
our condition of distress, what help could she have
offered ? What could she have done for us in such a
sea as was now running ? Yet the mere sight of her
had heartened me. She made me feel that help could
never be wanting in an ocean so ploughed by keels as
the Atlantic.

I crawled down on to the quarterdeck, and returned
to the Captain's cabin. The poor man at once fell
with feverish eagerness to questioning me. I told

him honestly that the maintopgallant-mast had carried away while I was on deck, but that there was nothing else wrong that I could distinguish ; that the barque was still making a noble fight, though there were times when the seas broke very fiercely and dangerously over the forecastle.

He wagged his head with a gesture of distress, crying : ' So it is ! so it is ! One spar after another, and thus may we go to pieces !'

I told him of the great steam frigate that had passed, but to this piece of news he listened with a vacant look, and apparently could think of nothing but his spars. He asked in a childish, fretful way how long Helga had been below, and I answered him stoutly, ' Not nearly long enough for sleep.'

' Ay,' cried he, ' but the barque needs to be pumped, sir.'

' Your daughter will work the better for rest,' said I ; and then looking at my watch, I found it was time to give him his physic.

He exclaimed, looking at the wineglass, ' There is no virtue in this stuff ! The sufferer can make but one use of it.' And, still preserving a manner of curious childishness, he emptied the contents of the glass over the edge of his cot on to the deck, and, as he swung, lay watching the mess of it on the floor with a smile. I guessed that expostulation would be fruitless, and, indeed, having but very little faith myself in any sort of physic, I secretly applauded his behaviour.

I sat down upon the locker, and leaning my back against the bulkhead, endeavoured, by conversation, to bring a cheerful look to his countenance ; but his mood of depression was not to be conquered. At times he would ramble a little, quote passages from Danish plays in his native tongue, then pause with his head on one side, as though waiting for me to applaud what he forgot I did not understand.

' How fine is this from " Palnatoke " !' he would cry, or, ' Hark to this from that noble performance " Hacon Yarl"! Ah, it is England alone can match Oehlenschläger.'

I could only watch him mutely. Then he would break away to bewail his spars again, and to cry out that Helga would be left penniless, would be a poor beggar-girl, if his ship foundered.

' But is not the *Anine* insured ?' said I.

'Yes,' he answered; 'but not by me. I was obliged to borrow money upon her, and she is insured by the man who lent me the money.'

'But you have an interest in the cargo, Captain Nielsen?'

'Ay,' cried he, 'and that I insured; but what will it be worth to my poor little Helga?' And he hid his face in his hands and rocked himself.

However, he presently grew somewhat composed, and certainly more rational, and after awhile I found myself talking about Tintrenale, my home and associations, my lifeboat excursions, and the like; and then we conversed upon the course that was to be adopted should the weather moderate and find us still afloat. 'We should be able to do nothing,' he said, 'without assistance from a passing ship,' in the sense of obtaining a few sailors to work the barque; or a steamer might come along that would be willing to give us a tow.

'The Land's End cannot be far off,' said he.

'No,' said I, 'not if this gale means to drop to-day. But it will be far enough off if it is to go on blowing.'

He inquired what I made the drift to be, and then calculated that the English coast would now be bearing about east-north-east, sixty miles distant. ' Let the wind chop round,' cried he, with a gleam in his sunken eye, ' and you and Helga would have the *Anine* in the Channel before midnight.'

We continued to talk in this strain, and he seemed to forget the wretchedness of our situation; then suddenly he called out to know the time, abruptly breaking away from what he was saying.

' Hard upon eleven o'clock,' said I.

' This will not do!' he cried. ' The barque, as we talk, is filling under our feet. The well should be sounded. Helga must be called. I beseech you to call Helga,' he repeated nervously, smiting the side of his cot with his clenched hand. ' Ah, God !' he added, ' that I should be without the power to move !'

' I will sound the well,' said I. ' Should I find an increase, I will arouse your daughter.'

' Go, I beg of you !' he cried, in high notes. ' The barque seems sodden to me. She does not lift and fall as she did.'

I guessed this to be imagination ; but the mere

fancy of such a thing being true frightened me also, and I hastily went out. I dried the rod and chalked it as Helga had, and, watching my chance, dropped it, and found five inches of water above the level our last spell at the pump had left in the hold. I was greatly startled, and to make sure that my first cast was right, I sounded a second time, and sure enough the rod showed five inches, as before. I hastened with the news to the Captain.

'I knew it! I feared it!' he cried, his voice shrill with a very ecstasy of hurry, anxiety, and sense of helplessness that worked in him. 'Call Helga!—lose not an instant—run, I beg you will run!'

'But run where?' cried I. 'Where does the girl sleep?'

'Go down the hatchway in the deck-house,' he shouted in shrill accents, as though bent upon putting into this moment the whole of his remaining slender stock of vitality. 'There are four cabins under this deck. Hers is the aftermost one on the starboard side. Don't delay! If she does not instantly answer, enter and arouse her.' And as I sped from the cabin I heard him crying that he knew by the motions of

the ship she was filling rapidly, and that she would
go down on a sudden like lead.

It was a black, square trap of hatchway into which
I looked a moment before putting my legs over. There
was a short flight of almost perpendicular steps con-
ducting to the lower deck. On my descending I found
the place so dark that I was forced to halt till my
eyes should grow used to the obscurity. There was
a disagreeable smell of cargo down here, and such a
heart-shaking uproar of straining timbers, of creaking
bulkheads, of the thumps of seas, and the muffled,
yearning roar of the giant waters sweeping under the
vessel, that for a little while I stood as one utterly
bewildered.

Soon, however, I managed to distinguish outlines,
and, with outstretched hands and wary legs, made my
way to the cabin Captain Nielsen had indicated, and
beat upon the door. There was no response. I beat
again, listening, scarcely thinking, perhaps, that the
girl would require a voice as keen as a boatswain's
pipe to thread the soul-confounding and brain-
muddling clamour in this after-deck of the storm-
beaten barque. 'He bade me enter,' thought I, 'and

enter I must if the girl is to be aroused ;' and I turned the handle of the door and walked in.

Helga lay, attired as she had left the deck, in an upper bunk, through the porthole of which the daylight, bright with the foam, came and went upon her face as the vessel at one moment buried the thick glass of the scuttle in the green blindness of the sea, and then lifted it weeping and gleaming into the air. Her head was pillowed on her arm ; her hair in the weak light showed as though touched by a dull beam of the sun. Her eyes were sealed—their long lashes put a delicate shading under them ; her white face wore a sweet expression of happy serenity, and I could believe that some glad vision was present to her. Her lips were parted in the expression of a smile.

There was a feeling in me as of profanity in this intrusion, and of wrongdoing in the obligation forced upon me of waking her from a peaceful, pleasant, all-important repose to face the bitter hardships and necessities of that time of tempest. But for my single pair of arms the pump was too much, and she must be aroused. I lightly put my hand upon hers, and her smile was instantly more defined, as though my action were coincident with some phase of her dream. I pressed her hand; she sighed deeply, looked at me, and instantly sat up with a little frown of confusion.

'Your father begged me to enter and arouse you,' said I. 'I was unable to make you hear by knocking. I have sounded the well, and there is an increase of five inches.'

'Ah!' she exclaimed, and sprang lightly out of her bunk.

In silence and with amazing despatch, seeing that a few seconds before she was in a deep sleep, she put on her sea-helmet, whipped a handkerchief round her neck, and was leading the way to the hatch on buoyant feet.

On gaining the deck I discovered that the wrecked appearance of the ship aloft had been greatly heightened during my absence below by the foretopsail having been blown into rags. It was a single sail, and the few long strips of it which remained blowing out horizontally from the yards, stiff as crowbars, gave an indescribable character of forlornness to the fabric. Helga glanced aloft, and immediately perceived that the maintopgallant-mast had been wrecked, but said nothing, and in a minute the pair of us were hard at work.

I let go the brake only when my companion was too exhausted to continue ; but now, on sounding the well, we found that our labours had not decreased the water to the same extent as heretofore. It was impossible, however, to converse out of shelter ; moreover, a fresh danger attended exposure on deck, for, in addition to the wild sweeping of green seas forward, to the indescribably violent motions of the barque, which threatened to break our heads or our limbs for us, to fling us bruised and senseless against the bulwarks if we relaxed for a moment our hold of what was next us—in addition to this, I say, there was now the deadly menace of the topgallant-mast, with its weight of yards, fiercely swinging and beating right over our heads, and poised there by the slender filaments of its rigging, which might part and let the whole mass fall at any moment.

We entered the deck-house, and paused for a little while in its comparative silence and stagnation to exchange a few words.

'The water is gaining upon the ship, Mr. Tregarthen,' said Helga.

'I fear so,' I answered.

'If it should increase beyond the control of the pumps, what is to be done?' she asked. 'We are without boats.'

'What *can* be done?' cried I. 'We shall have to make some desperate thrust for life—contrive something out of the hencoop—spare booms—whatever is to be found.'

'What chance—what chance have we in such a sea as this?' she exclaimed, clasping her hands and looking up at me with eyes large with emotion, though I found nothing of fear in the shining of them or in the working of her pale face.

I had no answer to make. Indeed, it put a sort of feeling into the blood like madness itself even to *talk* of a raft, with the sound in our ears of the sea that was raging outside.

'And then there is my father,' she continued, 'helpless—unable to move—how is he to be rescued? I would lose my life to save his. But what is to be done if this gale continues?'

'His experience should be of use to us,' said I. 'Let us go and talk with him.'

She opened the door of the berth, halted, stared a minute, then turned to me with her forefinger upon her lip. I peered, and found the poor man fast asleep. I believed at first that he was dead, so still he lay, so easy was his countenance, so white too; but after watching a moment, I spied his breast rising and falling. Helga drew close and stood viewing him. A strange and moving sight was that swinging cot— the revelation of the deathlike head within, the swaying boyish figure of the daughter gazing with eyes of love, pity, distress at the sleeping, haggard face, as it came and went.

She sat down beside me. 'I shall lose him soon,' said she. 'But what is killing him? He was white and poorly yesterday; but not ill as he is now.'

It would have been idle to attempt any sort of encouragement. The truth was as plain to her as to me. I could find nothing better to say than that the gale might cease suddenly, that a large steam-frigate had passed us a little while before, that some vessel was sure to heave into sight when the weather moderated, and that meanwhile our efforts must be directed to keeping the vessel afloat. I could not again talk of the raft ; it was enough to feel the sickening tossing of the ship under us to render the thought of *that* remedy for our state horrible and hopeless.

The time slowly passed. It was drawing on to one o'clock. I went on deck to examine the helm and to judge of the weather; then sounded the well, but found no material increase of water. The barque, however, was rolling so furiously that it was almost impossible to get a correct cast. Before re-entering the house, I sent a look round from the shelter of the weather-bulwark, to observe what materials were to be obtained for a raft should the weather suffer us to launch such a thing, and the barque founder spite of our toil. There was a number of spare booms securely lashed on top of the seamen's deck-house and galley, and these, with the hencoop and hatch-covers, and the little casks or scuttle-butts out of which the men drank would provide us with what we needed. But the contemplation of death itself was not so dreadful to me as the prospect which this fancy of a raft opened. I hung crouching under the lee of the tall bulwark, gnawing my lip as thought after thought arose in me, and digging my finger-nails into the palms of my hands. The suddenness of it all! The being this time yesterday safe ashore, without the dimmest imagination of what was to come—the anguish of my poor old mother—the perishing, as I did not doubt, of my brave comrades of the lifeboat—then, this vessel slowly taking in water, dying as it were by inches, and as doomed as though Hell's curse were upon her, unless the gale should cease and help come !

I could not bear it. I started to my feet with a sense of madness upon me, with a wild and dreadful desire in me to show mercy to myself by plunging and by silencing the delirious fancies of my brain in the wide sweep of seething waters that rushed from the very line of the rail of the barque as she leaned to her beam-ends in the thunderous trough of that instant. It was a sort of hysteria that did not last; yet might I have found temptation and time in the swift passage of it to have destroyed myself, but for God's hand upon me, as I choose to believe, and to be ever thankful for.

CHAPTER VII.

THE RAFT.

How passed the rest of this the first day of my wild and dangerous adventure, of Helga's and my first day of suffering, peril, and romantic experience, I cannot clearly recall. A few impressions only survive. I remember returning to the deck-house and finding the captain still sleeping. I remember conversing with Helga, who looked me very earnestly in the face when I entered, and who, by some indefinable influence of voice and eye, coaxed me into speaking of my fit of horror on deck. I remember that she left me to obtain some food, which, it seems, was kept in one of the cabins below, and that she returned with a tin of preserved meat, a little glass jar of jam, a tin of biscuits, and a bottle of red wine like to what we had before drunk—a very pleasant, well-flavoured claret; that all the while we ate, her father slept, which made her happy, as she said he needed rest, not having closed his eyes for three nights and days, though it was wonderful to me that he should have fallen asleep in such a mood of excitement and of consternation as I had left him in; but as to his slumbering amid that uproar of straining timbers and flying waters, it is enough to say that he was a seaman.

I also recollect that throughout the remainder of the day we worked the pump at every two hours or thereabouts; but the water was unmistakably gaining upon the barque, and to keep her free would have needed the incessant plying of the pumps—both pumps at once — by gangs of fellows who could relieve one another and rest between. Helga told me that her father had given orders for a windmill pump to be rigged, Scandinavian fashion, but that there had been some delay, so the barque sailed without it. I said that no windmill pump would have stood up half an hour in such a gale of wind as was blowing; but all the same, I bitterly lamented that there was nothing of the sort aboard, for these windmill arrangements keep the pumps going by the revolution of their sails, and such a thing must have proved inexpressibly valuable when the weather should moderate, so as to allow us to erect it.

The Captain slept far into the afternoon, but I could not observe when he awoke that he was the better for his long spell of rest. I entered his cabin fresh from a look round on deck, and found him just awake, with his eyes fixed upon his daughter, who sat slumbering upon the locker, with her back against the cabin-wall and her pale face bowed upon her breast. He immediately attacked me with questions, delivered in notes so high, penetrating, and feverish with hurry and alarm that they awoke Helga. We had to tell him the truth—I mean, that the water was gaining, but slowly, so that it must conquer us if the gale continued, yet we might still hope to find a chance of our lives by keeping the pump going. He broke into many passionate exclamations of distress and grief, and then was silent, with the air of one who abandons hope.

'There are but two, and one of them a girl,' I heard him say, lifting his eyes to the deck above as he spoke.

The night was a dreadful time to look forward to. While there was daylight, while one could see, one's spirits seemed to retain a little buoyancy ; but, speaking for myself, I dreaded the effect upon my mind of a second interminable time of blackness, filled with the horrors of the groaning and howling gale, of the dizzy motion of the tormented fabric, of the heart-subduing noises of waters pouring in thunder and beating in volcanic shocks against and over the struggling vessel.

Well, there came round the hour of nine o'clock by my watch. Long before, after returning from a spirit-breaking spell of toil at the pump, we had lighted the deck-house and binnacle lamps, had eaten our third meal that day to answer for tea or supper, and at Helga's entreaty I had lain down upon the deck-house locker to sleep for an hour or so if I could, while she went to watch by her father and to keep an eye upon the ship by an occasional visit to the deck.

We had arranged that she should awaken me at nine, that we should then apply ourselves afresh to the pump, that she should afterwards take my place upon the locker till eleven, I, meanwhile, seeing to her father and to the barque, and that we should thus proceed in these alternations throughout the night. It was now nine o'clock. I awoke, and was looking at my watch when Helga entered from the deck. She came up to me and took my hands, and cried :

' Mr. Tregarthen, there are some stars in the sky. I believe the gale is breaking !'

Only those who have undergone the like of such experiences as these I am endeavouring to relate can conceive of the rapture, the new life, her words raised in me.

' I praise God for your good news !' I cried, and made a step to the barometer to observe its indications.

The rise of the mercury was a quarter of an inch, and this had happened since a little after seven. Yet, being something of a student of the barometer in my little way, I could have heartily wished the rise much more gradual. It might betoken nothing more than a drier quality of gale, with nothing of the old fierceness wanting. But then, to be sure, it might promise a shift, so that we stood a chance of being blown homewards, which would signify an opportunity of preservation that must needs grow greater as we approached the English Channel.

I went with Helga on deck, and instantly saw the stars shining to windward betwixt the edges of clouds which were flying across our mastheads with the velocity of smoke. The heaven of vapour that had hung black and brooding over the ocean for two days was broken up ; where the sky showed it was pure, and the stars shone in it with a frosty brilliance. The atmosphere had wonderfully cleared ; the froth glanced keenly upon the hurling shadows of the seas, and I believed I could follow the clamorous mountainous breast of the ocean to the very throb of the horizon, over which the clouds were pouring in loose masses, scattering scud-like as they soared, but all so plentiful that the heavens were thick with the flying wings.

But there was no sobering of the wind. It blew with its old dreadful violence, and the half-smothered barque climbed and plunged and rolled amid clouds of spray in a manner to make the eyes reel after a minute of watching her. Yet the mere sight of the stars served as a sup of cordial to us. We strove at the pump, and then Helga lay down ; and in this manner the hours passed till about four o'clock in the morning, when there happened a sensible decrease in the wind. At dawn it was still blowing hard, but long before this, had we had sailors, we should have been able to expose canvas, and start the barque upon her course.

I stood on top of the deck-house watching the dawn break. The bleak gray stole over the frothing sea and turned ashen the curve of every running surge. To windward the ocean-line went twisting like a corkscrew upon the sky and seemed to boil and wash along it as though it were the base of some smoking wall. There was nothing in sight. I searched every quarter with a passionate intensity, but there was nothing to be seen. But now the sea had greatly moderated, and, though the deck still sobbed with wet, it was only at long intervals that the foam flew forwards. The barque looked fearfully wrecked, stranded and sodden. All her rigging was slack, the decks were encumbered with the ends of ropes, the weather side of the main-sail had blown loose and was fluttering in rags, though to leeward the canvas lay furled.

I went on to the quarter deck and sounded the well. Practice had rendered me expert, and the cast, I did not doubt, gave me the true depth, and I felt all the blood in me rush to my heart when I beheld such an indication of increase as was the same as hearing one's funeral knell rung, or of a verdict of death pronounced upon one.

I entered the deck-house with my mind resolved, and seated myself at the table over against where Helga lay sleeping upon the locker, to consider a little before arousing her. She showed very wan, almost haggard, by the morning light; her parted lips were pale, and she wore a restless expression even in her sleep. It might be that my eyes being fixed upon her face aroused her; she suddenly looked at me, and then sat up. Just then a gleam of misty sunshine swept the little windows.

'The bad weather is gone!' she cried.

'It is still too bad for us, though,' said I.

'Does the wind blow from the land?' she asked.

'Ay! and freshly too.'

She was now able to perceive the meaning in my face, and asked me anxiously if anything new had

happened to alarm me. I answered by giving her the
depth of water I had found in the hold. She clasped
her hands and started to her feet, but sat again on my
making a little gesture.

'Miss Nielsen,' said I, 'the barque is taking in
water very much faster than we shall be able to pump
it out. We may go on plying the pump, but the
labour can only end in breaking our hearts and
wasting precious time that might be employed to
some purpose. We must look the truth in the face,
and make up our minds to let the vessel go, and
to do our best, with God's help, to preserve our
lives.'

'What?' she asked in a low voice, that indicated
awe rather than fear, and I noticed the little twitch
and spasm of her mouth swiftly vanish in an expression of resolution.

'We must go to work,' said I, 'and construct a raft,
then get everything in readiness to sway it overboard.
The weather may enable us to do this. I pray so. It
is our only hope, should nothing to help us come
along.'

'But my father?'

'We shall have to get him out of his cabin on to the raft.'

'But how? But how?' she cried with an air of wildness. 'He cannot move!'

'If we are to be saved, he must be saved, at all events,' said I. 'What, then, can be done but to lower him in his cot, as he lies, on to the deck and so drag him to the gangway and sling him on to the raft by a tackle?'

'Yes,' she said, 'that can be done. It will have to be done.' She reflected, with her hands tightly locked upon her brow. 'How long do you think,' she asked, 'will the *Anine* remain afloat if we leave the pumps untouched?'

'Your father will know,' said I. 'Let us go to him.'

Captain Nielsen sat erect in his cot munching a biscuit.

'Ha!' he cried as we entered. 'We are to have pleasant weather. There was some sunshine upon that port just now. What says the barometer, Mr. Tregarthen?' then contracting his brows while he peered at his daughter as though he had not obtained a view of her before, he exclaimed, 'What is the matter, Helga? What have you come to tell me?'

'Father,' she answered, sinking her head a little and so looking at him through her eyelashes, 'Mr. Tregarthen believes, and I cannot doubt it, for there is the sounding-rod to tell the story, that water is fast entering the *Anine*, and that we must lose no time to prepare to leave her.'

'What!' he almost shrieked, letting fall his biscuit and grasping the edge of the cot with his emaciated hands, and turning his body to us from the waist, leaving his legs in their former posture as though he were paralyzed from the hip down. 'The *Anine* sinking? prepare to leave her? Why, you have neglected the pump, then!'

'No, Captain, no,' I answered. 'Our toil has been as regular as we have had strength for. Already your daughter has done too much; look at her!' I cried, pointing to the girl. 'Judge with your father's eye how much longer she is capable of holding out!'

'The pump must be manned!' he exclaimed, in such another shrieking note as he had before delivered. 'The *Anine* must not sink; she is all I have in the world. My child will be left to starve! Oh, she has strength enough. Helga, the gentleman does not know your strength and courage! And you, sir, —you, Mr. Tregarthen—Ach! God! You will not let your courage fail you—you who came here on a holy and beautiful errand—no, no! you will not let your courage fail you, now that the wind is ceasing and the sun has broken forth, and the worst is past?'

Helga looked at me.

'Captain Nielsen,' said I, 'if there were a dozen of us we might hope to keep your ship long enough afloat to give us a chance of being rescued; but not twelve, not fifty men could save her for you. The tempest has made a sieve of her, and what we have now to do is to construct a raft while we have time and opportunity, and to be ceaseless in our prayer that the weather may suffer us to launch it and to exist upon it until we are succoured.'

He gazed at me with a burning eye, and breathed as though he must presently suffocate.

'Oh, but for a few hours' use of my limbs!' he cried, lifting his trembling hands. 'I would show

you both how the will can be made to master the
body's weakness. Must I lie here without power?'
and as he said these words he grasped again the
edge of his cot, and writhed so that I was almost
prepared to see him heave himself out; but the agony
of the wrench was too much; his face grew whiter
still, he groaned low, and lay back, with his brow
glistening with sweat-drops.

'Father!' cried Helga, 'bear with us! Indeed it
is as Mr. Tregarthen says. I feared it last night,
and this morning has made me sure. We must not
think of the ship, but of ourselves, and of you, father
dear—of you, my poor, dear father!' She broke off
with a sob.

I waited until he had recovered a little from the
torment he had caused himself, and then gently, but
with a manner that let him know I was resolved,
began to reason with him. He lay apparently
listening apathetically; but his nostrils, wide with
breathing, and the hurried motions of his breast were
warrant enough of the state of his mind. While I
addressed him Helga went out, and presently returned with the sounding-rod, dark with the wet fresh

from the well. He turned his feverish eyes upon it, but merely shook his head and lightly wrung his hands.

'Father, you see it for yourself!' she cried.

'Miss Nielsen,' said I, 'we are wasting precious minutes. Will your father tell you what depth of water his ship must take in to founder?'

He, poor fellow, made no response, but continued to stare at the rod in her hand as though his intelligence on a sudden was all abroad.

'Shall we go to work?' said I. She looked at her father wistfully. 'Come,' I exclaimed, 'we *know* we are right. We must make an effort to save ourselves. Are not our lives our first consideration?'

I stepped to the door; as I put my hand to it, Captain Nielsen cried: 'If you do not save the ship, how will you save yourselves?'

'We must at once put some sort of raft together,' said I, halting.

'A raft! in this sea!' he clasped his hands and uttered a low mocking laugh that was more shocking in him than the maddest explosion of temper could have shown.

I could no longer linger to hear his objections. Helga might be very dear to him, but his ship stood first in his mind, and I had no idea of breaking my heart at the pump and then of being drowned after all. My hope was indeed a forlorn one, but it was a hope for all that; whereas I knew that the ship would give us no chance whatever. Besides, our making ready for the worst would not signify that we should abandon the vessel until her settling forced us over the side. And was the gentle, heroic Helga to perish without a struggle on my part, because her father clung with a sick man's craziness—which in health he might be quick to denounce — to this poor tempest-strained barque that was all he had in the world ?

I went out and on to the deck, and was standing thinking a minute of the raft and how we should set about it, when Helga joined me.

' He is too ill to be reasonable,' she exclaimed.

' Yes,' said I, ' but we will save him and ourselves too, if we can. Let us lose no more time. Do you observe that the wind has sensibly decreased even while we have been talking in your father's cabin?

The sky has opened more yet to windward, and the seas are running with much less weight.'

As I spoke the sun flashed into a rift in the vapour sweeping down the eastern heaven, and the glance of the foam to the splendour, and the sudden brightening of the cloud-shadowed sea into blue, animated me like some new-born hope, and was almost as invigorating to my spirits as though my eyes had fallen upon the gleam of a sail heading our way.

I should but weary you to relate, step by step, how we went to work to construct a raft. The motion of the deck was still very violent, but it found us now as seasoned as though we had kept the sea for years; and, indeed, the movement was becoming mere child's-play after the tossing of the night. A long hour of getting such booms as we wanted off the sailors' house on to the deck, and of collecting other materials for our needs, was not, by a very great deal, so exhausting as ten minutes at the pump. We broke off a little after nine o'clock to get some food, and to enable Helga to see to her father; and now the cast we took with the sounding-rod advised us, with most bitter significance of indication, that, even

though my companion and I had strength to hold to
the pump for a whole watch—I mean for four hours
at a spell—the water would surely, if but a little more
slowly, vanquish us in the end.   Indeed, there was no
longer question that the vessel had, in some parts of
her, been seriously strained ; and though I held my
peace, my sincere conviction was that, unless some
miracle arrested the ingress of the water, she would
not be afloat at five o'clock that day.

By one we had completed the raft, and it lay
against the main hatch, ready to be swayed over the
side and launched.   I had some small knowledge of
boat-building, having acquired what I knew from a
small yard down past the lifeboat-house at Tintrenale,
where boats were built, and where I had killed many
an hour, pipe in mouth, watching and asking questions, and even lending a hand ; and in constructing
this raft I found my slender boat-building experiences very useful.   First we made a frame of four
stout studdingsail booms, which we securely lashed to
four empty casks, two of which lay handy to our use,
while of the other two, one we found in the galley,
half full of slush, and the other in the cabin below

where the provisions were stored. We decked the frame with booms, of which there was a number, as I have previously said, stacked on top of the sailors' deck-house, and to this we securely lashed planking, to which we attached some hatch-covers, binding the whole with turn upon turn of rope. To improve our chance of being seen, I provided for setting up a topgallant-studdingsail boom as a mast, at the head of which we should be able to show a colour. I also took care to hedge the sides with a little bulwark of life-lines lest the raft should be swept. There were many interstices in this fabric fit for holding a stock of provisions and water.

I had no fear of its not floating high, nor of its not holding together : but it would be impossible to express the heaviness of heart with which I laboured at this thing. The raft had always been the most dreadful nightmare of the sea to my imagination. The stories of the sufferings it had been the theatre of were present to my mind as I worked, and again and again they would cause me to break off and send a despairing look round ; but never a sail showed ; the blankness was that of the heavens.

We had half-masted a second Danish ensign after coming out from breaking our fast, and one needed but to look at the breezy rippling of its large folds to know that the wind was rapidly becoming scant. By one o'clock, indeed, it was blowing no more than a pleasant air of wind, still out of the north-east. The stormy, smoke-like clouds of the morning were gone, and the sky was now mottled by little heaps of prismatic vapour that sailed slowly under a high delicate shading of cloud, widely broken, and showing much clear liquid blue, and suffering the sun to shine very steadily. There was a long swell rolling out of the north-east; but the brows were so wide apart that there was no violence whatever in the swaying of the barque upon it. The wind crisped these swinging folds of water, and the surface of the ocean scintillated with lines of small seas feathering, with merry curlings, into foam. But it was fine-weather water, and the barometer had risen greatly, and I could now believe that there was nothing more in the rapidity of its indications than a promise of a pleasant day and of light winds.

I could have done nothing without Helga. Her

activity, her intelligence, her spirit, were amazing, not
indeed only because she was a girl, but because she
was a girl who had undergone a day and two frightful
nights of peril and distress, who had slept but little,
whose labours at the pump might have exhausted a
seasoned sailor. She seemed to know exactly what
to do, was wise in every suggestion, and I could never
glance at her face without finding the sweetness of it
rendered noble by the heroism of the heart that
showed in her firm mouth, her composed countenance,
and steadfast, determined gaze.

At times we would break off to sound the well, and
never without finding a fresh nimbleness coming into
our hands and feet, a wilder desire of hurry penetrating our spirits from the assurance of the rod.
Steadily, inch by inch, the water was gaining, and
already at this hour of one o'clock it was almost easy
to guess the depth of it by the sluggishness of the
vessel's rolling, by the drowning character of her
languid recovery from the slant of the swell. I felt
tolerably confident, however, that she would keep
afloat for some hours yet, and God knows we could
not have too much time granted to us, for there was

much to be done ; the raft to be launched and pro-
visioned ; and the hardest part was yet to come, I
mean the bringing of the sick captain from his cabin
and hoisting him over the side.

At one o'clock we broke off again to refresh ourselves with food and drink, and Helga saw to her
father. For my part I would not enter his berth. I
dreaded his expostulations and reproaches, and,
indeed, I may say that I shrank from even the sight
of him, so grievous were his white face and dying
manner—so depressing to me, who could not look at
the raft and then turn my eyes upon the ocean without guessing that I was as fully a dying man as he,
and that, when the sun set this night, it might go
down for ever upon us.

There was but one way of getting the raft over, and
that was by the winch and a tackle at the mainyard-
arm. Helga said she would take the tackle aloft, but
I ran my eye over her boy-clad figure with a smile,
and said ' No.' She was, indeed, a better sailor than
I, but it would be strange indeed if I was unable to
secure a block to a yardarm. We braced in the
mainyard until the arm of it was fair over the gang-

way, and I then took the tackle aloft and attached the block by the tail of it.

I lay over the yard for a minute or two while I looked round ; but the sea brimmed unbroken towards the sky, and I descended again and again shuddering without control over myself, as I gazed at the little fabric of the raft and contrasted it with the size of the ship that was slowly foundering, and then with the great sea upon whose surface it would presently be afloat—the only object, perhaps, under the eye of heaven for leagues and leagues !

Our business now was to get the raft over the side. I should have to fatigue and perhaps perplex you with technicalities exactly to explain our management of it. Enough if I say that, by hooking on the lower block of the tackle to ropes which formed slings for the raft, and by taking the hauling part to the winch, we very easily swayed the structure clear of the bulwark-rail—for you must know that the winch, with its arrangements of handles, cogs, and pawls, is a piece of ship-board mechanism with which a couple of persons may do as much as a dozen might be able to achieve using their arms only.

When the raft was high enough Helga stood by the winch ready to slacken away on my giving the word of command ; while I went to a line which held the fabric over the deck. This line I eased off until the raft had swung fairly over the water, and then called to Helga to slacken away, and the raft sank, and in a minute or two was water-borne, riding upon the swell alongside, and buoyed by the casks even higher above the surface than I had dared hope.

' Now, Miss Nielsen !' cried I.

' Oh ! pray call me Helga,' she broke in ; ' it is my name : it is short ! I seem to answer to it more readily, and in this time, this dreadful time, I could wish to have it, and none other !'

' Then, Helga,' said I, even in such a moment as this feeling my heart warm to the brave, good, gentle little creature as I pronounced the word, ' we must provision the raft without delay. Our essential needs will be fresh water and biscuit. What more have you in your provision-room below ?'

' Come with me !' said she, and we ran into the deck-house and descended the hatch, leaving the raft securely floating alongside, not only in the grip of the yardarm tackle, which the swaying of the vessel had fully overhauled, but in the hold of the line with which we had slacked the structure over the rail.

It was still dark enough below; but when we opened the door of the berth in which, as I have told you, the cabin provisions were stowed, we found the sunshine upon the scuttle or porthole, and the apartment lay clear in the light. In about twenty minutes, and after some three or four journeys, we had conveyed on deck as much provisions as might serve to keep three persons for about a month : cans of meat, some hams, several tins of biscuit, cheese, and other matters, which I need not catalogue. But we had started the fresh water in the scuttle-butts that they might be emptied to serve as floats for the raft, and now we had to find a cask or receptacle for drinking-water, and to fill it, too, from the stock in the hold. Here I should have been at a loss but for Helga, who knew where the barque's fresh water was stowed. Again we entered the cabin or provision-room, and returned with some jars whose contents we emptied—vinegar, I believe it was, but the hurry my mind was then in rendered it weak in its reception of.

small impressions ; these we filled with fresh water from a tank conveniently stowed in the main hatch-way, and as I filled them Helga carried them on deck.

While we were below at this work I bade her listen.

'Yes, I hear it !' she cried : ' it is the water in the hold.'

With every sickly lean of the barque you could hear the water inside of her seething among the cargo as it cascaded now to port and now to star-board.

'Helga, she cannot live long,' said I. 'I believe, but for the hissing of the water, we should hear it bubbling into her.'

I handed her up the last of the jars, and grasped the coaming of the hatch to clamber on to the deck, for the cargo came high. As I did this, something seemed to touch and claw me upon the back, and a huge black rat of the size of a kitten leapt from my shoulder on to the deck and vanished in a breath. Helga screamed, and indeed, for the moment, my own nerves were not a little shaken, for I distinctly felt the wire-like whisker of the horrible creature brush my cheek as it sprang from my shoulder.

'If there be truth in the proverb,' said I, 'we need no surer hint of what is coming than the behaviour of that rat.'

The girl shuddered, and gazed, with eyes bright with alarm, into the hold, recoiling as she did so. I believe the prospect of drifting about on a raft was less terrible to her than the idea of a second rat leaping upon one or the other of us.

CHAPTER VIII.

ADRIFT.

IT was necessary that we should have everything in readiness before we carried poor Captain Nielsen out of his cabin. I unshipped the gangway, and watching an opportunity as the swell lifted the raft against the side of the barque stooping to it, I sprang; but I could not have imagined the weight and volume of the swell until I had gained the frail platform. Indeed, one could feel that the wrath kindled by the tempest still lived in the deep bosom of the ocean. It was like a stern, revengeful breathing; but the wind was light, and the water but delicately brushed, and it was easy to foresee that if no more wind blew the swell would have greatly flattened down by sunset. Yet the manner in which the hull and the raft came together terrified me with a notion of our contrivance going to pieces. I called to Helga, as she threw to me or handed the several parcels and articles we had collected upon the deck, that there was not a moment of time to waste—that we must get her father on to the raft without delay; and then, when I had hastily stowed the last of the things, I sprang aboard again, and was going straight to the Captain's berth, when I suddenly stopped, and exclaimed : ' First, how is he to be removed ?'

She eyed me piteously. Perhaps her seamanship did not reach to *that* height ; or maybe her fear that we should cause her father pain impaired her perception of what was to be done.

' Let me think, now,' said I. ' It is certain that he must be lowered to the deck as he lies in his cot. Does he swing by hooks ? I did not observe.'

' Yes,' she answered, ' what you would call the clews come together to a point as in a hammock, and spread at the foot and head.'

' Then there must be iron eyes in the upper deck,' cried I, ' to receive the hooks. Now, see here ! we shall have to get a sling at each end of the cot, attach a line to it, the ends of which we will pass

through the eyes, and when this is done we will cut
away the clews, and so lower him.   Yes, that will do,'
said I.   ' I have it,' and, looking about me for such a
thickness of rope as I needed, I overhauled some
fathoms, passed my knife through the length, and together we hastened to the Captain's berth.

' What is it now ?' he asked, in a feeble voice, as we
entered.

' Everything is ready, Captain Nielsen,' said I
' there is no time to lose.   The cargo is washing
about in the hold, and the ship has not another hour
of life left in her.'

' What is it that you want ?' said he, looking dully
at the coil of rope I held in my hand.

' Father, we are here to carry you to the raft.'

' To the raft !' he exclaimed, with an air of bewilderment, and then he added, while I noticed a little
colour of temper enter his cheeks.   ' I have nothing
to do with your raft.   It was in your power to save
the poor *Anine.*   If she is to founder, I will go down
with her.'

So saying, he folded his arms upon his bosom in a
posture of resolution, viewing me with all the severity

his sickness would suffer his eyes to express. Nevertheless, there was a sort of silliness in the whole manner of him which might have persuaded the most heedless observer that the poor fellow was rapidly growing less and less responsible for his behaviour. Had he been a powerful man, or, indeed, possessed the use of his extremities, I should have dreaded what is termed a 'scene.' As it was, nothing remained but to treat him as a child, to tackle him with all tenderness, but as swiftly as possible, and to get him over the side.

There was a dreadful expression of distress in Helga's face when she looked at him; but her glances at me were very full of assurance that she was of my mind, and that she would approve and be with me in sympathy in whatever I resolved to do. Whipping out my knife, I cut lengths off the rope I held to make slings off. I carried one of these slings to the cot and passed it over the end. The Captain extended his hand, and attempted to thrust me aside. The child-like weakness of that trembling push would, in a time of less wretchedness and peril than this, have unnerved me with pity.

'Bear with me! Be yourself, Captain! Show yourself the true Danish sailor that you are at heart —for Helga's sake !' I exclaimed.

He covered his eyes and sobbed.

I secured the slings to the cot, and, until we lowered him to the deck, he held his face hidden in his hands. I rove two lengths of line through the iron eyes at which the cot slung. in the manner I had described to Helga, and when the weight of the cot was on these lines, we belayed one end, holding by the other. I then passed my knife through the clews, as it would be called, or thin lines which supported the cot, and, going to the rope I had belayed, bade Helga lower her end as I lowered mine, and the cot descended safely to the deck. The girl then came round to the head of the cot, and together we dragged it out of the house on to the deck.

Saving a little wrench when we hauled the cot over the coaming of the deck-house door, the poor man was put to no pain. It was merciful indeed that he should have lain ill in the deck-house, for had he occupied a cabin below I cannot imagine how we should have got him out on to the deck without killing him with the anguish which we should have been forced by our efforts to cause him.

When we had got him to the gangway I sprang on to the raft and caught hold of the block that dangled at the extremity of the yardarm tackle. With this I returned to the barque, and, just as we had got the raft over, so did we sway the poor Captain on to her. I got on to the raft to receive him as Helga lowered the cot. He descended gently, and on my crying, ' Let go !' she swiftly released the line, and the tackle overhauled itself to the roll of the vessel.

I remember exclaiming ' Thank God !' when this job was ended, and I had unhooked the block, as though the worst was over ; and indeed, in the mere business of abandoning the barque, the worst had ended with the bestowal of the sick and helpless Captain on the raft. But what was now to begin ? My ' Thank God !' seemed to sound like a piece of irony in my heart when I looked from the deep, wet, gleaming side of the leaning hull, waving her wrecked spars in the reddening light of the sun—when I looked from her, I say, to seawards, where the flowing lines of the lifting and falling swell were running bald and foamless into the south-west sky.

Helga came to the gangway and called to know if all were well with her father.

'All is well,' I answered. 'Come now, Helga! There is nothing to detain us. We shall be wise to cast adrift from the barque. She is very much down by the head, and the next dip may be her last.'

'A few minutes cannot signify,' she cried. 'There are one or two things I should like to bring with me. I wish to possess them, if we are preserved.'

'Make haste, then!' I called. She disappeared, and I turned to the Captain. He looked up at me out of his cot with eyes in which all the feverish fire of the morning was quenched.

'Is Helga remaining in the barque?' he asked listlessly.

'God forbid!' cried I. 'She will be with us in a minute or two.'

'It is a cruel desertion,' said he. 'Poor *Anine!* You were to have been kept afloat!'

It was idle to reason with him. He was clothed as I had found him when I had first seen him—in a waistcoat and serge coat, and a shawl round his neck ; but he was without a hat—a thing to be overlooked at such a time as this—and the lower part of him was protected only by the blankets he lay under. There was still time to supply his requirements. I had noticed his wideawake and a long cloak hanging in his berth, and I immediately sprang on board, rushed aft, procured them and returned. Helga was still below. I put the hat on the Captain's head and clasped the cloak over his shoulders, fretting over the girl's absence, for every minute was communicating a deadlier significance to the languid, sickly, dying motions of the fast-drowning hull.

I think about ten minutes had passed since she left the barque's side to go to her cabin, when, bringing my eyes away from the sea, into whose eastern quarter I had been gazing with some wild hope or fancy in me of a sail down there—though it proved no more than a feather-tip of cloud—I saw Helga in the gangway. I say Helga, but for some moments I did not know her. I started and stared as if she had been a ghost. Instead of the boyish figure to which my sight was already used, there stood in the aperture

betwixt the bulwarks, which we call the gangway, a
girl who looked at least half a head taller than the
Helga who had been my associate. I might have
guessed at once that this appearance of stature in her
was due to her gown, but, as I did not suspect that
she had gone to change her dress, her suggestion of
increased height completed the astonishment and
perplexity with which I regarded her. She stood on
the leaning and swaying side of the barque, as perfect
a figure of a maiden as mortal eyes could wish to rest
on. Her dress was of a dark-blue serge that clung to
her : she also wore a cloth jacket, thinly edged about
the neck and where it buttoned with fur, and upon
her head was a turban-shaped hat of sealskin, the
dark glossy shade of which brightened her short hair
into a complexion of the palest gold. She held a
parcel in her hand, and called to me to take it from
her. I did so, and cried :

'You will not be able to jump from the gangway.
Get into the fore-chains, and I will endeavour to haul
the raft up to you.'

But even as I spoke she grasped her dress, and
disclosed her little feet, and with a bound gained the

raft as it rose with the swell, yielding on her knees as she struck the platform with the grace that nothing but the teaching of old ocean could have communicated to her limbs.

' Thank God you are here !' I cried, catching her by the hand. ' I was growing uneasy—in another minute I should have sought you.'

She faintly smiled, and then turned eagerly to her father.

' I have my mother's portrait,' said she, pointing to the parcel, ' and her Bible. I would not bring away more. If we are to perish, they will go with us.'

He looked at her with a lack-lustre eye, and in a low voice addressed a few words to her in Danish. She answered in that tongue, glancing down at her dress, and then at me, and added, in English, ' It was time, father. The hard work is over. I may be a girl now ;' and looking along the sea she sighed bitterly.

Her father brought his knitted hands together to his brow, and never could I have imagined the like of the look of mental anguish that was on his face as he did this. But what I am here narrating did not occupy above a minute or two. Indeed, a longer delay than this was not to have been suffered if we desired the raft to hold together. I let go the line that held the little structure to the barque, and getting the small studding-sail boom over—that is, the boom we had shipped to serve as a signal-mast—I thrust with it, and, Helga helping me, we got the raft clear of the side of the vessel. The leewardly swell on which we rode did the rest for us, and not a little rejoiced was I to find our miserable fabric gradually increasing its distance from the *Anine ;* for if the barque foundered with us close alongside, we stood to be swamped in the vortex, the raft scattered, and ourselves left to drown.

It now wanted about twenty minutes to sundown. A weak air still blew, but the few clouds that still lived in the heavens floated overhead apparently motionless ; yet the swell continued large, to our sensations at least, upon that flat structure, and the slope of the platform rapidly grew so distressing and fatiguing to our limbs, that we were glad to sit and obtain what refreshment we could from a short rest.

Among the things we had brought with us was the bull's-eye lamp, together with a can of oil, a parcel of meshes, and some lucifer-matches. I said to Helga :

' We should step, or set up, our mast before it grows dark.'

' Why ?' she inquired. ' The flag we hoist will not be seen in the dark '—knowing that the mast was there for no other purpose than to display a flag on.

' But we ought to light the lamp and masthead it,' said I, ' and keep it burning all night—if God suffers us to live through the night. Who can tell what may come along ?—what vessel invisible to us may perceive the light ?'

She answered quickly : ' Yes. Your judgment is clearer than mine. I will help you to set up the mast.'

Her father again addressed her in Danish. She answered him, and then said to me, ' My father asks why we are without a sail.'

' I thought of a sail,' I replied, speaking as I went about to erect the mast, ' but without wind it could not serve us, and with wind it would blow away like a cobweb. It would have occupied too much time to rig and securely provide for a sail. Besides, our hopes could never lie in the direction of such a thing. We must be picked up—there is no other chance for us.'

The Captain made no response, but sat, propped up on his pillows, motionless, his eyes fixed upon the barque.

The sun had sunk, but a strong scarlet yet glowed in the western sky by the time we had erected and stayed the spar. I then lighted the lamp and ran it aloft by means of a line and a little block which I had taken care to throw into the raft. This finished, we seated ourselves.

There was now nothing more to be done but watch and pray. This was the most solemn and dreadful moment that had as yet entered into the passage of our fearful and astonishing experience. In the hurry and agitation of leaving the barque there had been scarcely room for pause. All that we could think of was how quickly to get away, how speedily to equip and launch the raft, how to get Captain Nielsen over, and the like; but all this was ended : we could now think—and I felt as if my heart had been suddenly crushed in me as I sat on the slanting, falling, and rising platform viewing the barque, that lay painted in clear black lines against the fast-dimming glow in the west.

Helga sat close against her father's cot. So far as I was able to distinguish her face, there was profound grief in it, and a sort of dismay, but no fear. Her gaze was steady, and the expression of her mouth firm. Her father kept his eyes rooted upon his ship. I overheard her address him once or twice in Danish, but getting no reply, she sighed heavily and held her peace. I was too exhausted in body and spirits to desire to speak. I remember that I sat, or rather squatted, Lascar fashion, upon the hatch-cover, that somewhat raised the platform of the raft, with my hands clasped upon my shins, and my chin on a level with my knees, and in this posture I continued for some time motionless, watching the *Anine*, and waiting for her to sink, and realizing our shocking situation to the degree of that heart-crushing sensation in me which I have mentioned. I was exactly clad as I had been when I boarded the barque out of the lifeboat. Never once, indeed, from the hour of my being in the vessel, down to the present moment, had I removed my oilskins, saving my sou'-wester, which I would take from my head when I entered the cabin; and I recollect thinking that it was better for me to be heavily than thinly clad, because being a stout swimmer, a light dress would help me to a bitter long battle for life, whereas the clothes I had on must make the struggle brief, and speedily drag me down into peace, which was, indeed, all that I could bring my mind to dwell upon now, for when I sent my glance from the raft to the darkling ocean, I felt hopeless.

The rusty hectic died out. The night came along in a clear dusk with a faint sighing of wind over the raft every time the swell threw her up. There was a silver curl of moon in the south-west, but she was without power to drop so much as a flake of her light into the dark shadow of water under her. Yet the starlight was in the gloom, and it was not so dark but that I could see Helga's face in a sort of glimmer, and the white outline of the cot and the configuration of the raft upon the water in dusky strokes.

The barque floated at about a cable's length distant from us, a dark mass, rolling in a strangling manner, as I might know by the sickly slide of the stars in the

squares of her rigging and along the pallid lines of
the canvas stowed upon her yards. There was more
tenacity of life in her than I should have believed
possible, and I said to Helga :

'If this raft were a boat, I would board the barque
and set her on fire. She may float through the night,
for who is to know but that one of her worse leaks may
have got choked, and the blaze she would make might
bring us help.'

The Captain uttered some exclamation in Danish,
in a small but vehement and shrill tone. He had not
spoken for above an hour, and I had believed him
sleeping or dying and speechless.

' What does he say?' I called across softly to Helga.

' That the *Anine* might have been saved had we
stood by her,' she answered, struggling, as I could
hear by the tremor in her voice, to control her
accents.

'No, no!' said I, almost gruffly, I fear, with the
mood that was upon me of helplessness, despair, and
the kind of rage that comes with perception that one
is doomed to die like a rat, without a chance, without
a soul of all those one loves knowing one's fate. 'No,

no !' I cried, ' the *Anine* was not to be saved by us
two, nor by twenty like us, Helga. *You* know that—
for it is like making me responsible for our situation
here to doubt it.'

' I do not doubt it,' she answered firmly and re-
proachfully.

Captain Nielsen muttered in his native tongue ;
but I did not inquire what he said, and the hush of
the great ocean night, with its delicate threading of
complaining wind, fell upon us.

My temper of despair was not to be soothed by
recollection of this time yesterday, by perception of
the visible evidence of God's mercy in this tranquillity
of sky and sea, at a time when, but for the change of
weather, we had certainly been doomed. I was young ;
I passionately desired to live. Had death been
the penalty of the lifeboat attempt, I might, had time
been granted me, contemplated my end with the forti-
tude that springs from the sense of having done well.
But what was heroic in this business had disappeared
out of it when the lifeboat capsized and left me safe
on board. It was now no more than a vile passage
of prosaic shipwreck, with its attendant horror of

lingering death, and nothing noble in what had been done, or that might yet have to be done, to prop up my spirits. Thus I sat, full of wretchedness, and miserably thinking, mechanically eyeing the dusky heap of barque ; then breaking away from my afflicting reverie, I stood up, holding by the mast, to carefully sweep the sea, with a prayer for the sight of the coloured gleams of a steamer's lights, since there was nothing to be expected in the way of sail in this calm that was upon the water.

I was thus occupied, when I was startled by a strange cry—I cannot describe it. It resembled the moan of a wild creature wounded to death, but with a human note in it that made the sound something not to be imagined. For an instant I believed it came from the sea, till I saw by the dim light of the starshine the figure of Captain Nielsen, in a sitting-posture, pointing with the whole length of his arm in the direction of his barque. I looked, and found the black mass of hull gone, and nothing showing but the dark lines of spars and rigging that melted out of my sight as I watched. A noise of rending, intermingled with the shock of an explosion, came from where she had disappeared. It signified no more than the blowing up of the decks as she sank ; but the star-studded vastness of gloom made the sound appalling beyond language to convey.

' Help !' cried Helga. ' My father is dying.'

I gained the side of the cot in a stride, and kneeled by him, but there was no more to be seen of his face than the mere faint whiteness of it, and I could not tell whether his eyes were open or not. Imagining, but scarcely hoping, that a dram might put some life into the poor fellow, I lowered the bull's-eye lamp from the masthead to seek for one of the jars of spirits we had stowed ; but when we came to put the tin panni-kin to his lips we found his teeth set.

' He is not dead, Helga,' I cried ; 'he is in a fit. If he were dead his jaw would drop ;' and this I sup-posed, though I knew little of death in those days.

I flashed the bull's-eye upon his face, and observed that though his eyes were open the pupils were up-turned and hidden. This, with the whiteness of the skin and the emaciation of the lineaments, made a ghastly picture of his countenance, and the hysteric sob that Helga uttered as she looked made me grieve that I should have thrown the light upon her father.

I mastheaded the lamp again, and crouched by the side of the cot talking to Helga across the recumbent form in it. Who could remember what was said at such a time? I weakly essayed to cheer her, but soon gave up, for here was the very figure of Death himself lying between us, and there was Death awaiting us in the black invisible folds in which we swung; and what had I to say that could help her heart at such a time? Occasionally I would stand erect and peer around. The weak wind that went moaning past us as the raft rose to the liquid heave, had the chill in it of the ocean in October; and fearing that Helga's jacket did not sufficiently protect her, I pulled off my oilskin-coat—there is no warmer covering for ordinary apparel—and induced her to put it on. Her father remained motionless, but by stooping my ear to his mouth I could catch the noise of his breathing as it hissed through his clenched teeth. Yet it was a sort of breathing that would make one expect to hear it die out in a final sigh at any minute.

I mixed a little spirit and water, and gave it to the girl, and obliged her to swallow the draught, and begged her to eat for the sake of the life and heart food would give her ; but she said ' No,' and her frequent silent sobbing silenced me on that head, for how could one grieving as she did swallow food ? I filled the pannikin for myself and emptied it, and ate a biscuit and a piece of cheese, which were near my hand in an interstice of the raft, and then lay down near the cot, supporting my head on my elbow. Never did the stars seem so high, so infinitely remote, as they seemed to me that night. I felt as though I had passed into another world that ·mocked the senses with a few dim semblances of things which a little while before had been real and familiar. The very paring of moon showed small as though looked at through an inverted telescope, and measurelessly remote. I do not know why this should have been, yet once afterwards, in speaking of this experience to a man who, in a voyage to India, had fallen overboard on such another night as this, and swam for three hours, he told me that the stars had seemed to him as to me, and the moon, which to him was nearly full, appeared to have shrunk to the size of the planet Venus.

After awhile the Captain's breathing grew less harsh, and Helga asked me to bring the lamp that she might look at him. His teeth were no longer set, and his eyes as in nature, saving that there was no recognition in them, and I observed that he stared straight into the brilliant glass of magnified flame without winking or averting his gaze. I propped him up, and Helga put the pannikin to his lips, but the fluid ran from the corners of his mouth ; upon which I let him rest upon his pillows, softly begging the girl to let God have His way with him.

'He cannot last through the night !' she exclaimed, in a low voice ; and the wonderful stillness upon the sea, unvexed by the delicate winnowing of the draught, gathered to my mood an extraordinary emphasis from my being able to hear her light utterances as distinctly as though she whispered in a sick-room.

'You are prepared, Helga?' said I.

'No, no !' she cried, with a little sob. 'Who can

be prepared to lose one that is dearly loved? We believe we are prepared—we pray for strength; but when the blow falls it finds us weak and unready. When he is gone, I shall be alone. And, oh! to die *here!*'

We sank into silence.

Another hour went by, and I believed I had fallen into a light, troubled doze, less sleepful than a waking daydream, when I heard my name pronounced, and instantly started up.

'What is it?' I cried.

'My father is asking for you,' answered Helga.

I leaned over the cot and felt for his hand, which I took. It was of a death-like coldness, and moist.

'I am here, Captain Nielsen,' said I.

'If God preserves you,' he exclaimed, very faintly, 'you will keep your word?'

'Be sure of it—be sure of it,' I said, knowing that he referred to what had passed between us about Helga.

'I thank you,' he whispered. 'My sight seems dark; yet is not that the moon down there?'

'Yes, father,' answered the girl.

'Helga,' he said, 'did you not tell me you had brought your mother's likeness with you?'

'It is with us, and her Bible, father.'

'Would to God I could look upon it,' said he, 'for the last time, Helga—for the last time!'

'Where is the parcel?' I asked.

'I have it close beside me,' she answered.

'Open it, Helga!' said I. 'The lamp will reveal the picture.'

Again I lowered the bull's-eye from the masthead, and, while Helga held the picture before her father's face, I threw the light upon it. It was a little oil-painting in an oval gilt frame. I could distinguish no more than the face of a woman—a young face—with a crown of yellow hair upon her head. The sheen of the lamp lay faintly upon the profile of Helga. All else, saving the picture, was in darkness, and the girl looked like a vision upon the blackness behind her, as she knelt with the portrait extended before her father's face.

He addressed her in weak and broken tones in Danish, then turned his head and slightly raised his arm, as though he wished to point to something up in the sky, but was without power of limb to do so. On this Helga withdrew the portrait, and I put down the lamp, first searching the dark line of ocean, now scintillant with stars, before sitting again.

As the moon sank, spite of her diffusing little or no light, a deeper dye seemed to come into the night. The shooting-stars were plentiful, and betokened, as I might hope, continuance of fair weather. Here and there hovered a steam-coloured fragment of cloud. An aspect of almost summer serenity was upon the countenance of the sky, and though there was the weight of the ocean in the swing of the swell, there was peace too in the regularity of its run and in the soundless motion of it as it took us, sloping the raft after the manner of a see-saw.

In a boat, aboard any other contrivance than this raft put together by inexpert hands, I must have felt grateful—deeply thankful to God indeed, for this sweet quietude of air and sea that had followed the roaring conflict of the long hours now passed. But I was without hope, and there can be no thankfulness without that emotion. These were the closing days of October; November was at hand; within an hour this sluggish breathing of air might be storming up into such another hurricane as we were fresh from. And what then? Why, it was impossible to fancy such a thing even, without one's spirits growing heavy as lead, without feeling the presence of death in the chill of the night air.

No! for this passage of calm, God forgive me! I could not feel grateful. The coward in me rose strong. I could not bless Heaven for what affected me as a brief pause before a dreadful end, that this very quiet of the night was only to render more lingering, and fuller, therefore, of suffering.

Captain Nielsen began to mutter. I did not need to listen to him for above a minute to gather that he was delirious. I could see the outline of Helga against the stars, bending over the cot. The thought of this heroic girl's distress, of her complicated anguish, rallied me, and I broke in a very passion of self-reproach from the degradation of my dejection. I drew to the cot, and Helga said :

' He is wandering in his mind.' She added, with a note of wailing in her voice, ' Jeg er nu alene ! Jeg er nu alene !' by which she signified that she was now alone. I caught the meaning of the sentence from her pronunciation of it, and cried :

' Do not say you are alone, Helga ! Besides, your father still lives. Hark ! what does he say ?'

So far he had been babbling in Danish ; now he spoke in English, in a strange voice that sounded as though proceeding from someone at a distance.

' It is so, you see. The storks did not return last spring. There was to be trouble !—there was to be trouble ! Ha ! here is Pastor Madsen. Else, my beloved Else ! here is the good Pastor Madsen. And there, too, is Rector Grönlund. Will he observe us ? Else, he is deep in his book. Look !' he cried a little shrilly, pointing with a vehemence that startled me into following the indication of his shadowy glimmering hand directed into the darkness over the sea. ' It is Kolding Latin School—nay, it is Rector Grönlund's parsonage garden. Ah, Rector, you remember me ? This is the little Else that your good wife thought the prettiest child in Denmark. And this is Pastor Madsen.'

He paused, then muttered in Danish, and fell silent.

CHAPTER IX.

RESCUED.

THIS is a thing easy to recall, but how am I to convey the reality of it? What is there in ink to put before you that wide scene of starlighted gloom, the dusky shapes of swell for ever running noiselessly at us—no sounds save the occasional creaking of the raft as she was swayed—the motionless, black outlines of Helga and myself overhanging the pallid streak of cot—at intervals a low sob breaking from the girl's heart, and the overwhelming sense of present danger, of hopelessness, made blacker yet by the night? And amid all this the crazy babbling of the dying Dane, now in English and now in his native tongue!

It was just upon the stroke of one o'clock in the morning when he died. I had brought my watch to the lamp, when he fetched a sort of groaning breath, of a character that caused me to bend my ear to his lips : and I found that he had ceased to breathe. I continued to listen, and then, to make sure, cast the light of the lamp upon him.

'He has gone!' cried Helga.

'God has taken him,' said I. 'Come to this side, and sit by me!'

She did as I asked, and I took her hand. I knew by her respiration that she was weeping, and I held my peace till her grief should have had some vent. I then spoke of her father, represented that his ailments must in all probability have carried him off almost as swiftly ashore ; that he had died a peaceful death, with his daughter beside him, and his wife and home present in a vision to his gaze ; and said that, so far from grieving, we should count it a mercy that he had been called away thus easily, for who was to imagine what lay before us—what sufferings, which must have killed him certainly later on ?

'His heart broke when his barque sank,' said she. 'I heard it in his cry.'

This might very well have been too.

Never was there so long a night. The moon was behind the sea, and after she was gone the very march of the stars seemed arrested, as though nature had cried 'Halt!' to the universe. Having run the lamp aloft, I resolved to leave it there, possessed now with such a superstitious notion as might well influence a shipwrecked man, that if I lowered it again no vessel would appear. Therefore, to tell the time, I was obliged to strike a match, and whenever I did this I would stare at my watch and put it to my ear and doubt the evidence of my sight, so inexpressibly slow was the passage of those hours.

Helga's sobs ceased. She sat by my side, speaking seldom after we had exhausted our first talk on her coming round to where I was. I wished her to sleep, and told her that I could easily make a couch for her, and that my oilskin would protect her from the dew. I still held her hand as I said this, and I felt the shudder that ran through her when she replied that she could not lie down, that she could not sleep. Perhaps she feared I would disturb her father's body to make a bed for her; and, indeed, there was nothing on the raft, but the poor fellow's cloak

and his pillows and blankets, out of which I could
have manufactured a bed.

Had I been sure that he was dead, I should have
slipped the body overboard while it remained dark,
so that Helga should not have been able to see what
I did ; but I had not the courage to bury him merely
because I believed he was dead, because he lay there
motionless ; and I was constantly thinking how I
should manage when the dawn came—how I was so
to deal with the body as to shock and pain poor
Helga as little as possible.

As we sat side by side, I felt a small pressure of
her shoulder against my arm, and supposed that she
had fallen asleep, but, on my whispering, she immediately answered. Dead tired I knew the brave girl
must be, but sleep could not visit eyes whose gaze I
might readily guess was again and again directed at
the faint pale figure of the cot.

The light air shifted into the north-west at about
three o'clock in the morning, and blew a small breeze
which extinguished the star-flakes that here and there
rode upon the swell, and raised a noise of tinkling,
rippling waters along the sides of the raft. I guessed

this new direction of the wind by my observation of a bright greenish star which had hung in the wake of the moon, and was now low in the west. This light breeze kindled a little hope in me, and I would rise again and again to peer into the quarter whence it blew, in the expectation of spying some pale shadow of ship. Once Helga, giving a start, exclaimed :

'Hush! I seem to hear the throb of a steamer's engines !'

We both stood up hand in hand, for the sway of the raft made a danger of it as a platform, and I listened with strained hearing. It might have been a steamer, but there was no blotch of darkness upon the obscurity the sea-line round to denote her, nor any gleam of lantern. Yet for nearly a quarter of an hour did we listen, in a torment of attention, and then resumed our seats side by side.

The dawn broke at last, dispelling, as it seemed to my weary despairing imagination, a long month of perpetual night. The cold gray was slow and stealthy, and was a tedious time in brightening into the silver and rose of sunrise. My first act was to sweep the sea for a ship, and I then went to the cot and looked at the face upon the pillows in it. If I had never seen death before, I might have known it now. I turned to the girl.

'Helga,' said I gently, 'you can guess what my duty is—for your sake, and for mine, and for his too.'

I looked earnestly at her as I spoke : she was deadly pale, haggard, her eyes red and inflamed with weeping, and her expression one of exquisite touching sorrow and mourning. But the sweetness of her young countenance was dominant even in that supreme time, and, blending with the visible signs of misery in her looks, raised the mere prettiness of her features into a sad beauty that impressed me as a spiritual rather than as a physical revelation.

'Yes, I know what must be done,' she answered. 'Let me kiss him first.'

She approached the cot, knelt by it, and put her lips to her father's : then raising her clasped hands above her head, and looking upwards, she cried out : '*Jeg er faderlös! Gud hjelpe mig !*'

I stood apart waiting, scarcely able to draw my breath for the pity and sorrow that tightened my throat. It is impossible to imagine the plaintive wailing note her voice had as she uttered those Danish words : '*I am fatherless! God help me!*' She then hid her face in her hands, and remained kneeling and praying.

After a few minutes she arose, kissed again the white face, and seated herself with her back upon the cot.

No one could have named to me a more painful, a more distasteful piece of work than the having to handle the body of this poor Danish captain, and launch him into that fathomless grave upon whose surface we lay. First I had to remove the ropes which formed our little bulwark, that I might slide the cot overboard ; then with some ends of line I laced the figure in the cot, that it should not float away out of it when launched. The work kept me close to the body, and, thin and white as he was, yet he looked so lifelike, wore an expression so remonstrant, that my horror was sensibly tinctured with a feeling of guilt, as though instead of burying him I was about to drown him.

I made all despatch possible for Helga's sake, but came to a pause, when the cot was ready, to look about me for a sinker. There was nothing that I could see but the jars, and, as they contained our little stock of spirits and fresh water, they were altogether too precious to send to the bottom. I could do no more than hope that the canvas would speedily grow saturated, then fill and sink; and, putting my hands to the cot, I dragged it to the edge of the raft, and went round to the head and pushed.

It was midway over the side, when a huge black rat sprang from among the blankets out through the lacing, and disappeared under the hatch-cover. I had no doubt it was the same rat that had leapt from my shoulder aboard the barque. If it had terrified me there, you will guess the shock it caused me now! I uttered some cry in the momentary consternation raised in me by this beastly apparition of life flashing, so to speak, out of the very figure and stirlessness of death, and Helga looked and called to know what was the matter.

'Nothing, nothing,' I replied. 'Turn your eyes from me, Helga!'

She immediately resumed her former posture,

covering her face with her hands. The next moment
I had thrust the cot fair into the sea, and it slid off to
a distance of twice or thrice its own length, and lay
rising and falling, to all appearances buoyant as the
raft itself. I knew it would sink so soon as the
canvas and blankets were soaked, yet that might take
a little while in doing, and dreading lest Helga should
look—for you will readily conceive how dreadful
would be to the girl that sight of her father afloat in
the square of canvas, his face showing clearly through
the lacing of rope—I went to her, and put my arm
round her, and so, but without speaking, obliged her
to keep her face away. I gathered from her passive-
ness that she understood me. When I glanced again,
the cot was in the act of sinking; in a few beats of
the heart it vanished, and all was blank ocean to the
heavens—a prospect of little flashful and feathering
ripples, but glorious as molten and sparkling silver in
the east under the soaring sun.

I withdrew my hand from Helga's shoulder. She
then looked, and sighed heavily, but no more tears
flowed. I believe she had wept her heart dry!

'In what words am I to thank you for your kindness and sympathy?' said she. 'My father and my mother are looking down upon us, and they will bless you.'

'We must count on being saved, Helga,' said I, forcing a cheerful note into my voice. 'You will see Kolding again, and I shall hope to see it too, by your side.' And, with the idea of diverting her mind from her grief, I told her of my promise to her father, and how happy it would make me to accompany her to Denmark.

'I have been too much of a home bird,' said I. 'You will provide me with a good excuse for a ramble, Helga ; but first you shall meet my dear old mother, and spend some time with us   I am to save your life, you know.   I am here for that purpose ;' and so I continued to talk to her, now and again coaxing a light sorrowful smile to her lips ; but it was easy to know where her heart was ; all the while she was sending glances at the sea close to the raft, where she might guess the cot had sunk, and twice I overheard her whisper to herself that same passionate, grieving sentence she had uttered when she kissed her father's dead face : '*Jeg er faderlös ! Gud hjelpe mig !*'

The morning stole away. Very soon after I had buried the Captain I lowered the lamp, and sent the Danish flag we had brought with us to the head of the little mast, where it blew out bravely, and promised to boldly court any passing eye that might be too distant to catch a sight of our flat platform of raft. I then got breakfast, and induced Helga to eat and drink. Somehow, whether it was because of the sick complaining Captain, with his depressing menace of death, being gone, or because of the glad sunshine, the high marbling of the heavens, full of fine weather, and the quiet of the sea, with its placid heave of swell and its twinkling of prismatic ripples, my heart felt somewhat light, my burden of despondency was easier to carry, was less crushing to my spirits. What to hope for I did not know. I needed no special wisdom to guess that if we were not speedily delivered from this raft we were as certainly doomed as though we had clung to the barque and gone down in her. Yet spite of this there was a stirring of hope in me. It seemed impossible but that some ship must pass us before the day was gone. How far we had blown to the southward and westward during the gale I could not have told, but I might be sure we were not very distant from the mouth of the English Channel, and therefore in the fair way of vessels inward and out-ward bound, more particularly of steamers heading for Portuguese and Mediterranean ports.

But hour after hour passed, and nothing hove into view. The sun went floating from his meridian into the west, and still the horizon remained a blank, near, heaving line, with the sky whitening to the ocean rim. Again and again Helga sought the boundary, as I did. Side by side we would stand, she holding by my arm, and together we gazed, slowly sweeping the deep.

' It is strange !' she once said, after a long and thirsty look. ' We are not in the middle of the ocean. Not even the smoke of a steamer !'

' Our horizon is narrow,' answered I. ' Does it exceed three miles ? I should say not, save when the swell lifts us, and then, perhaps, we may see four. Four miles of sea !' I cried. ' There may be a dozen ships within three leagues of us, all of them easily within sight from the maintop of the *Anine,* were she afloat. But what, short of a straight course for the raft, could bring this speck of timber on which we stand into view? This is the sort of situation to make one understand what is signified by the immensity of the ocean.'

She shivered and clasped her hands.

'That I—that we,' she exclaimed, speaking slowly and almost under her breath, 'should have brought you to this pass, Mr. Tregarthen! It was our fate by rights—but it ought not to be yours!'

'You asked me to call you Helga,' said I; 'and you must give me my Christian name.'

'What is it?' she asked.

'Hugh.'

'It is a pretty name. If we are spared, it will be sweet to my memory while I have life!'

She said this with an exquisite artlessness, with an expression of wonderful sweetness and gentleness in her eyes, which were bravely fastened upon me, and then, suddenly catching up my hand, put her lips to it and pressed it to her heart, letting it fall as she turned her face upon the water on that side of the raft where her father's body had sunk.

My spirits, which remained tolerably buoyant while

the sun stood high, sank as he declined. The prospect of another long night upon the raft, and of all
that might happen in a night, was insupportable. I
had securely bound the planks together, as I believed,
but the constant play of the swell was sure to tell after
a time. One of the ligatures might chafe through,
and in a minute the whole fabric scatter under our
feet like the staves of a stove boat, and leave us no
more than a plank to hold on by in the midst of this
great sea which all day long had been without ships.
I often bitterly deplored I had not brought a sail
from the barque, for the air that hung steady all day
blew landwards, and there was no weight in it to have
carried away the flimsiest fabric we could have erected.
A sail would have given us a drift—perhaps have put
us in the way of sighting a vessel, and in any case it
would have mitigated the intolerable sense of helpless imprisonment which came to one with thoughts
of the raft floating without an inch of way upon her,
overhanging all day long, as it might have seemed,
that very spot of waters in which Helga's father had
found his grave.

Shortly before sundown Helga sighted a sail in the

south-west. It was the merest shaft of pearl gleaming above the ocean rim, and visible to us only when the quiet heave of the sea threw us up. It was no more than a vessel's topmost canvas, and before the sun was gone the dim star-like sheen of those cloths had faded out into the atmosphere.

'You must get some rest to-night, Helga,' said I. 'Your keeping awake will not save us if we are to be drowned, and if we are to be saved then sleep will keep you in strength. It is the after-consequences of this sort of exposure and mental distress which are to be dreaded.'

'Shall I be able to sleep on this little rickety platform?' she exclaimed, running her eyes, glowing dark against the faint scarlet in the west, over the raft. 'It brings one so dreadfully near to the surface of the sea. The coldness of the very grave itself seems to come out of it.'

'You talk like a girl now that you are dressed as one, Helga. The hearty young sailor-lad that I met aboard the *Anine* would have found nothing more than a raft and salt water in this business, and would have " planked " it here as comfortably as in his cabin bunk.'

'It did not please you to see me in boy's clothes,' said she.

'You made a very charming boy, Helga ; but I like you best as you are.'

'No stranger should have seen me dressed so,' she exclaimed in a tone of voice that made me figure a little flush in her cheeks, though there was nothing to be seen in that way by the twilight which had drawn around us. 'I did not care what the mates and the crew thought, but I could not have guessed——' she stammered and went on : 'when I saw in the bay what the weather was likely to prove, I determined to keep my boy's dress on, more particularly after that wretched man, Damm, went away with the others, for then the *Anine* would be very short-handed for what might happen ; and how could I have been of use in this attire ?' and she took hold of her dress and looked down it.

'I have heard before,' said I, 'of girls doing sailors' work, but not for love of it. In the old songs and stories they are represented as

going to sea chiefly in pursuit of absconding sweet-
hearts.'

'You think me unwomanly for acting the part of a
sailor?' said she.

'I think of you, Helga,' said I, taking her by the
hand, 'as a girl with the heart of a lioness. But if I
once contrive to land you safely at Kolding, you will
not go to sea again, I hope?'

She sighed, without replying.

There was nothing but her father's cloak and my
oilskins to make a couch for her with. When I
pressed her to take some rest, she entreated softly
that I would allow her to go on talking and sitting
—that she was sleepless—that it lightened her heart
to talk with me—that there were many hours of
darkness yet before us—and that before she consented to lie down we must arrange to keep watch,
since I needed rest too.

I was willing, indeed, to keep her at my side talking. The dread of the loneliness which I knew would
come off the wide, dark sea into my brain when she
was silent and asleep, and when there would be
nothing but the stars and the cold and ghastly

gleam of the ebony breast on which we lay, to look
at, was strong upon me. I mastheaded the bull's-eye
lamp, and spread the poor Danish Captain's cloak,
and we seated ourselves upon it, and for a long two
hours we talked together, in which time she gave me
her life's history, and I chatted to her about myself.
I listened to her with interest and admiration. Her
voice was pure, with a quality of plaintive sweetness
in it, and now and again she would utter a sentence in
Danish, then translate it. It might be that the girlish
nature I now found in her was accentuated to my ap-
preciation by the memory of her boyish attire, by her
appearance when on board the barque, the work she
did there and the sort of roughness one associates
with the trade of the sea, whether true of the indi-
vidual or not; but, as I thought, never had I been in
the company of any woman whose conversation and
behaviour were so engaging, with their qualities
of delicacy, purity. simplicity, and candour, as
Helga's.

It was such another night as had passed, saving
that the ocean swell had the softness of the long
hours of fine weather in its volume, whereas on the

previous night it still breathed as in memory of the fierce conflict that was over.

A little after midnight there was a red scar of moon in the west, and the hour was a very dark one, spite of the silver showering of the plentiful stars. I had made for Helga the best sort of couch it was in my power to manufacture, and at this time she lay upon it sleeping deeply, as I knew by the regularity of her respiration. The sense of loneliness I dreaded had been upon me since she lay down and left me to the solitary contemplation of our situation. A small wind blew out of the north-west, and there was much slopping noise of waters under my feet amid the crevices of the clumsily framed raft. I had promised Helga to call her at three, but without intending to keep my word if she slept, and I sat near her head, her pale face glimmering out of the darkness as though spectrally self-luminous, and for ever I was turning my eyes about the sea and directing my gaze at the little masthead lantern to know that it was burning.

Happening to bend my gaze down upon the raft, into some interstice close against where the hatch-

cover was secured, I spied what, for the moment, I
might have supposed a pair of glow-worms, minute,
but defined enough. Then I believed there was a
little pool of water there, and that it reflected a couple
of stars. A moment after I guessed what it was, and
in a very frenzy of the superstition that had been
stirring in me, and in many directions of thought in-
fluencing me from the moment of my leaving the
barque, I had my hand upon the great rat—for that
was what it was—and sent it flying overboard. I remember the wild squeak of the thing as I hurled it—
you would have supposed it the cry of a distant gull.
There was a little fire in the water, and I could see
where it swam, and all very quietly I seized hold of a
loose plank and, waiting till it had come near, I hit
it, and kept on hitting it, till I might be sure it was
drowned.

Some little noise I may have made : Helga spoke
in her sleep, but did not wake. You will smile at
my mentioning this trifling passage ; you would
laugh could I make you understand the emotion of
relief, the sense of exultant happiness, that possessed
me when I had drowned this rat. When I look back

and recall this little detail of my experiences, I never doubt that the overwhelming spirit of the loneliness of that ocean night lay upon me in a sort of craziness. I thought of the rat as an evil spirit, a something horribly ominous to us, a menace of suffering and of dreadful death while it stayed with us. God knows why I should have thus thought ; but the imagination of the shipwrecked is quickly diseased, and the moods which a man will afterwards look back upon with shame and grief and astonishment are, while they are present, to him as fruitful of terrible imaginings as ever made the walls of a madhouse ring with maniac laughter.

It might have been some half-hour after this—the silly excitement of the incident having passed out of my mind—that I fell into a doze. Nature was wellnigh exhausted in me, yet I did not wish to sleep. In proportion, however, as the workings of my brain were stealthily quieted by the slumberous feelings stealing over me, so the soothing influences without operated : the cradling of the raft, the hushing and subduing gaze of the stars, the soft whispering of the wind.

I was awakened by a rude shock, followed by a
hoarse bawling cry. There was a second shock of a
sort to smartly bring my wits together, attended with
several shouts, such as—' What is it ? What have ye
run us into? Why, stroike me silly, if it ain't a raft!'

I sprang to my feet, and found the bows of a little
vessel overhanging us. Small as I might know her
to be, she yet loomed tall and black, and even
seemed to tower over us, so low-seated were we.
She lined her proportions against the starry sky, and
I made out that she had hooked herself to us by running her bowsprit through the stays which supported
our mast.

My first thought was for Helga, but she was rising
even as I looked, and the next moment was at my
side.

' For God's sake !' I cried, ' lower away your sail, or
your stem will grind this raft to pieces ! We are two
—a girl and a man—shipwrecked people. I implore
you to help us to get on board you !'

A lantern was held over the side, and the face of
the man who held it showed out to the touch of the
lustre like a picture in a *camera obscura*. The rays of

the lantern streamed fairly upon us, and the man
roared out :

' Ay ! it's a raft, Jacob, and there are two of 'em,
and one a gal. Chuck the man a rope's-end and he'll
haul the raft alongside.'

' Look out !' shouted another voice from the after-
part of the little vessel, and some coils of rope fell at
my feet.

I instantly seized the line, and, Helga catching hold
too, we strained our united weight at it, and the raft
swung alongside the craft at the moment that she
lowered her sail.

' Catch hold of the lady's hands !' I shouted.

In a moment she was dragged over the side. I
handed up the little parcel, containing her mother's
picture and Bible, and followed easily, scrambling over
the low rail.

The man who grasped the lantern held it aloft to
survey us, and I saw the dusky glimmer of two other
faces past him.

' This is a queer start !' said he. ' How long have
you been knocking about here ?'

' You shall have the yarn presently,' said I ; ' but

before the raft goes adrift, it's well you should know
that she is pretty handsomely stocked with provisions
—all worth bringing aboard.'

' Right !' he cried. ' Jacob, take this here lantern
and jump over the side, and hand up what ye find.'

All this had happened too suddenly to suffer me
as yet to be sensible of what came little short of a
miraculous deliverance ; for had the craft been a
vessel of burthen, or had there been any weight in
the soft night air still blowing, she would have sheared
through us as we lay asleep, and scattered the raft and
drowned us out of hand—nay, before we could have
cried ' O God !' we should have been suffocating in
the water.

I believed her at first a fishing-boat. She was
lugger-rigged and open, with a little forecastle in her
bows, as I had noticed while the lantern dangled in
the hand of the man who surveyed us. Yet, had she
been a line-of-battle ship, she could not, as a refuge
and a means of deliverance after the horror and peril
of that flat platform of raft, have filled me with more
joy and thanksgiving.

' The worst is over, Helga !' I cried, as I seized the

girl's cold and trembling hand. 'Here is a brave little vessel to carry us home, and you will see Kolding again, after all!'

She made some answer, which her emotion rendered scarcely intelligible. Her being suddenly awakened by the shock of the collision, her alarm on seeing what might have passed in the gloom as a tall, black mass of bow crushing into the raft; then the swiftness of our entry into the lugger, and the sensations which would follow on her perception of our escape from a terrible death—all this, combined with what she had gone through, was too much for the brave little creature; she could scarcely whisper; and, as I have said, her hand was cold as frost, and trembled like an aged person's, as I gently brought her to one of the thwarts.

By this time I had made out that the boat carried only three of a crew. One of them, holding the lantern, had sprung on to the raft, and was busy in handing up to the others whatever he could lay his hands upon. They did not spend many minutes over this business. Indeed, I was astonished by their despatch. The fellow on the raft worked like one who was very used to rummaging, and, as I knew afterwards by observing what he had taken, it was certain not a single crevice escaped him.

'That's all,' I heard him shout. 'There's naught left that I can find, unless so be as the parties have snugged any valuables away.'

'No!' I cried, 'there are no valuables, no money—nothing but food and drink.'

'Come aboard, Jacob, arter ye've chucked up what's loose for firewood.'

Presently the lantern flashed as it was passed across the rail, and the figure of the man followed.

'Shove her clear!' was bawled, and shortly afterwards, 'Up foresail!'

The dark square of sail mounted, and one of the men came aft to the helm. Nothing was said until the sheet had been hauled aft, and the little craft was softly rippling along over the smooth folds of the swell, communicating a sensation so buoyant, so vital after the flat mechanical swaying and slanting of the inert raft, that the mere feeling of it to me was as potent in virtue as some life-giving dram.

The other two men came out of the bows and seated

themselves, placing the lighted lantern in the midst of us, and so we sat staring at one another.

'Men,' said I, 'you have rescued us from a horrible situation. I thank you for my life, and I thank you for this lady's life.'

'How long have ye been washing about, sir?' said the man at the helm.

'Since Monday night,' said I.

'A bad job!' said he; 'but you'll have had it foine since Monday night. Anyone perish aboard your raft?'

'One,' I answered quickly. 'And now I'll tell you my story. But first I must ask for a drop of spirits out of one of those jars you have transhipped. A sudden change of this sort tries a man to the soul.'

'Ay, you're right,' growled one of the others. 'I know what it is to be plucked by the hair o' the head out of the hopen jaws of Death, and the sort of feelings what comes arter the plucking job's o'er. Which'll be the particler jar, sir?'

'Any one of them,' said I.

He explored with the lantern, found a little jar of brandy, and the glass, or rather I should say the pan-

a into taking a
side, as one still
t had happened.
you might have
self with her